P9-CAF-511

PRAISE FOR SUSAN DUNLAP AND HER "FEISTILY ATTRACTIVE PROTAGONIST"* BERKELEY HOMICIDE COP JILL SMITH

"Jill Smith is a welcome addition to the ranks of fictional
cops—a skilled investigator who is equally at home under-
cover on the colorful streets of Berkeley and in uniform in
her squad car. But Jill is more than a cool professional; she's
a contemporary woman coping with a contemporary woman's problems—be they dirty dishes in the sink or an ex-
husband who just won't let go."
—Marcia Muller, author of
There's Nothing to Be Afraid Of

"Dunlap has been called 'one of the Great Hopes of the
policewoman procedural novel.' With her latest book, [she]
has more than lived up to that hope."
—*The Sacramento Union*

"With two highly acclaimed detective series, Susan Dunlap
has carved out her own territory in the mystery field."
—*Mystery News*

"Dunlap is a quiet, clever, entertaining writer who keeps us
busily making the rounds with her protagonist and studying
the clues as they unfold."   —*San Francisco Chronicle*

"Once again Dunlap brings us bright and intelligent charac-
ters . . . this book is bound to please all mystery fans."
—*Ocala Star-Banner*

The New York Times Book Review

For Kareen Shepherd

1

"How about a gorilla?"

"Thanks a lot, Howard," I said, skirting a puddle. Seth Howard was six foot six, the tallest member of the Berkeley police force. I was nearly running to keep up with him. The rain pelted down—the first storm of the season. Yesterday it had been seventy degrees and sunny. At four-thirty today, it was pouring. Thunder rattled the sky, and stabs of lightning slashed at the treetops. Thunderstorms were a two-to-three-times-a-decade event in Berkeley, and for most people they were a free light show. No one here worried about whether to stand under trees or away from them. They headed for the spot where they could best see the lightning.

"If a gorilla suit isn't feminine enough, Jill, you could add a pink bow around your neck. Or maybe you should come as a skeleton in honor of your new job."

I didn't want to get into that: my promotion to Homicide and Howard's promotion to Special Investigations Bureau, which handled vice and drugs. His move should have been one that pleased Howard, and it did on every level, except that nothing could cover the fact that he had been passed over for the more prestigious Homicide job. Howard and I had been close friends for three years. We'd worked the same beat; we'd talked endlessly about everything from our cases to my divorce. We'd talked about our mutual ambition to someday be Chief of Police. But the Homicide job made a difference. I knew Howard well enough to realize he had been taken aback by the promotions, that he was appalled at resenting the good fortune of his close friend, appalled that he, like everyone else, could wonder if my being a woman had had anything to do with it. He was trying desperately— and failing—to react to me as he always had.

I didn't know how to handle the situation any better than he did. I said, "You're taking a lot of interest in my costume, Howard. You're the one who's giving this Halloween party. What are you going as?"

His thick, curly red hair hung in sopping ringlets that bounced heavily as he walked. He looked like a Raggedy Andy doll that had fallen in the bathtub. "Can't tell you about my costume. It's a surprise. But I will let you in on a little secret."

"What?"

"You'll never guess what it is."

"What makes you so sure?"

"It's very clever."

"Is that a challenge?"

"Could be." He sounded like the Howard of old, but there was more to this contest than just guessing his disguise. When we had been on beat together, neither of us would have turned down such a challenge. And I couldn't let it go now.

"What do I get if I figure out your costume?"

"Whatever you want. Let your fancy go wild because there is no way you'll guess."

"You're pretty smug. After all, I know what your decorations will be."

"Woolworth's best bones and goblins. Don't count on that too much."

"I know what you'll be serving."

"So you think I'll come as a chef?"

"I know who you've invited."

"Cops." He laughed. The light turned green. We started into the intersection. A van skidded to a halt. The streets were slick. After six dry months, drivers had forgotten how to maneuver in the rain. Some were high on grass or coke; most were mesmerized by the thunderstorm. It was a natural for accidents. I was glad not to be working traffic detail any longer.

My hair was caught at the nape of my neck so that much of the rain that hit my head was channeled along it and down the back of my jacket. But a sizable amount still managed to drip inside my collar. Neither Howard nor I had thought to bring umbrellas.

"Listen, how far away did you park?" Howard demanded. "We've already walked four blocks from the station."

"Two more blocks."

"If I'd known you were this far away, I would have taken the bus."

"If I could rent a garage like you do, right across from the station . . ."

"Maybe if you got to work a little earlier . . ." Howard was grinning.

"Howard," I said, tentatively.

Howard looked puzzled.

I could feel my smile becoming wider. "If I guess your costume, I can have anything I choose, is that right?"

Howard hesitated.

"That's what you said, right?"

"You'll never guess."

"Anything?"

"Yeah, anything."

"Okay. If I guess your costume before the party, you give me your garage lease."

I dropped Howard at the Co-op Garden Shop on Shattuck. Maybe he was planning to outfit himself as a tree. For him, it would have to be a redwood. Traffic was surprisingly light for quarter to five on a Thursday night. I drove on, heading toward the tunnel that ran under the Marin traffic circle and connected the extension of Shattuck Avenue at a right angle to Solano Avenue. If I could get to Solano before the majority of people got off work, I could find a parking spot near Ortman's and buy a pint of chocolate chocolate shower ice cream to have for dinner.

As I approached the tunnel, cars were stopped. There was generally a long line here, but tonight it was longer than usual. Even at this distance I could see the holdup. Over the tunnel, on the traffic circle, red lights flashed. There was no chance of turning till just before the tunnel, and now that right-hand turn that led, like a bent elbow, to the circle was closed off.

But my friend, Connie Periera, now had this beat. And even if she weren't the one handling this accident, the beat officer would let me through.

I pulled into the empty right lane that led to the blocked-off elbow and drove past glaring drivers waiting in the lane to my left. At the turn the patrol officer—young, black, and very wet—waved me to a stop.

"You see that line?" he snapped, as I opened the window of my old Volkswagen.

"I'm Smith, Homicide."

He glanced at the dented and rust-splotched fender of my car and back to my face. It was a moment before he nodded and said, "Homicide. Must be nice to deal with people when they're dead, when they don't give you no jive-assed excuses for cutting the line."

"Long day, huh?"

"Just beginning."

"Is Pereira in charge up there at the traffic circle?"

He smiled, a wistful, fleeting expression. Pereira was a popular blonde. "Yeah."

I started to ask what the accident was, but behind me a horn honked. "Let me through, okay?"

He looked at the line of cars. Shaking his head, he said,

"Okay, but every one of those turkeys in line is going to burn my ears about how you got through and they can't."

"Tell them my car wouldn't run long enough to wait in that tunnel line."

He glanced again at the dented fender and gave me a mock salute.

I shut the window and headed up the curve to the circle. I'd stop and see if Pereira needed an assist. When I'd been a beat officer and she a mere patrol officer, she had assisted me plenty. Even if it were a garden-variety fender bender, on a night like this another hand to move things along could save a lot of time.

Six streets crowd into the small residential traffic circle. Expensive homes sit on their corners. (One house is balanced directly atop the entrance to the tunnel beneath.) Cars with FOR SALE signs in their windows are parked around the outer edge. The circle is a demarcation point between the steep streets of the Berkeley hills and the gentler slope from there down toward San Francisco Bay.

But as I reached the circle, I could see that this was no mere fender bender. In the middle of the circle was an island of grass about thirty feet in diameter. The metal barrier that ran across that island was crushed to the ground. And the car that had done that, a silver Cadillac, had smashed into the decorative fencing at the outer edge of the circle. Had it not been for that sturdy cement fence, the car would have rolled into the living room of the house over the tunnel. Red lights flashed everywhere, blurring like finger painting in the rain.

As I pulled to the curb, I could see the ambulance lights in the distance. A patrol officer was diverting traffic below the circle—the pulser lights on his car flashed red. At the edge of the circle, small groups of bystanders stood under trees. Then I spotted Pereira. She was standing next to a tarpaulin-covered mound ten feet from the Cadillac. It had to be a body.

I walked over to her.

"Jill," she said. "It's good you're here." She bent down and lifted the tarp. "The driver, Ralph Palmerston."

He lay on his back, his arms bent in ways arms shouldn't go. His bloodstained shirt and jacket covered a chest that had been mashed out to the sides. The rain bounced off his face; it had matted his thick white hair and might have washed the blood from his face. Now there was surprisingly little; only a trickle caked at the side of his mouth and around his eyes—just enough to emphasize those blue eyes and their look of disbelief and horror.

The ambulance pulled up. Its red light flashed on and off Palmerston's face, turning it from red to ashen gray. In the stroboscopic unreality of the pulser light, it was like seeing the moment of the accident as Palmerston's terror-stricken face flung forward—then he hit the steering wheel and everything was covered with red.

As the ambulance men bent down, I turned away and looked toward the car. Misco, from Traffic Investigations, was huddled under the hood or what remained of it. Crinkled, it had been pushed back toward the empty windshield. On the Arlington, another of the feeder streets, a patrol officer diverted traffic.

The ambulance men prepared to lift the body. Pereira stepped back next to me. I said, "Were they a long time in coming? You must have been on the scene for a while— it's pretty well secured. Traffic Investigations is already here."

"Misco? That was just luck. He was only a block away when the call came in. But the ambulance"—she shook her head—"every ambulance in the area was out. It's the storm. I'm just glad there was no question about Palmerston. He was dead when I got here."

"How did it happen?"

"Witnesses say it looked like his brakes failed. He came down Marin. . . ." She glanced up across the circle to the extension of Marin Avenue that rose into the Berkeley Hills. It was the steepest street in the city. I hadn't been able to get my car up it in four years. And I knew people who went out of their way to avoid driving down it. "They said he was going sixty, seventy miles per hour. As far as we can tell, he ran the last two stop signs. He slammed into the divider and the car bounced—one hop—over here."

"Lucky no one was in his way."

"Very. He missed two witnesses by inches, or so they said. They're over there." She indicated a man and woman standing shock-stiff under a tree. Beyond them, on lower Marin Avenue, Lieutenant Davis, Pereira's watch commander, was getting out of his car.

"I'm glad you're here, Jill," Connie Pereira said.

"As long as you need me."

"It could be a long time."

I shrugged. "The tow truck's coming up the street."

Connie looked past me at a car pulling up. As the doors opened and the men got out, I could make out the print man from his bag, and the photographer. I looked quizzically at Connie.

"This isn't an accident, Jill. I thought so at first. It would have made sense. But that car was just serviced today. The sticker's on the door. The service report's in the glove compartment. Jill, you don't have a brake failure on a Cadillac three hours after it comes out of the shop."

2

The rain had let up a little, but another shaft of lightning burst from the sky, turning the traffic circle brighter than noon. In the sudden fluorescent glare, the crinkled metal of the Cadillac looked fragile, like a toy car that had been run over in the driveway.

Misco was sprawled under the car. Pereira stood with Lieutenant Davis and me, eyeing the access roads that led onto the circle lest any scofflaw invade her scene of the crime. Lieutenant Davis said nothing. The rain soaked my jacket.

"Aha!" Misco pushed himself free of the car and stood up. His brown hair was thinning on top. There was a streak of grease across his forehead. Misco was one of those men who had spent his adolescence under the hoods or bodies of a stream of used Chevys or Fords. In college he'd managed to husband his Saturdays for his vehicles. The one time I'd been to his house, he'd had two cars parked on the lawn and one on blocks in the driveway. For Misco, being in Traffic Investigations Unit was heaven.

"Perforations in the brake lines," he said. "You want to look?"

Eyeing the rain-soaked ground, Lieutenant Davis said, "Tell us about it first."

Momentarily Misco looked disappointed, but as soon

as he started to speak, his face brightened. "You should see the edges of the cuts where the brake fluid drained, Lieutenant. It's a great job."

"What do you mean by 'great job'?" I asked.

Pereira motioned us under the shelter of a London plane tree. Once there, Misco turned to me. "Do you know much about cars?"

"Nothing more than where to put the dip stick."

"Oh." He shot a look of distress at Lieutenant Davis. To me, he said, "Well, the simplest way I can put it is that if there are holes in the brake lines, the brake fluid seeps out and the brakes don't hold."

"That I understand. Anyone who watches television knows that."

"You said brake *lines,*" Lieutenant Davis prompted.

"Right. That's what makes this so interesting. A Cadillac has separate brake lines to the front and back wheels. It's a safety feature, so if the front brakes go, there are still the rear ones."

"But nothing held on this car," Pereira said.

"Because"—Misco could barely contain himself—"both lines were punctured. And the really impressive thing here is that the edges of the cuts are rough. If you weren't specifically looking for sabotage, you wouldn't even spot the cuts. The workmanship is good. No, it's nearly perfect. Any smaller cuts and the leaks would have been so gradual that the owner would have realized the brakes were going long before there was a serious problem. If the cuts were bigger, it wouldn't have taken an expert to find them."

"What you're saying," Lieutenant Davis said, "is that the perforations were just large enough for the brakes to go on Marin Avenue? If the car had come down another street, one not so steep, the driver would be okay; he just would have thought his brakes weren't holding like they should be, right?"

"That's it. The guy could have driven on the flatlands

for weeks, but on that hill, holding back thousands of pounds of Cadillac . . . well, you can see the pressure that puts on brakes."

I turned to Lieutenant Davis. "So you'll be passing this case on to Homicide?"

"You've seen the body and the scene, here, Smith," he said. "As soon as the paperwork is in order, it will be yours." He didn't add that he would be keeping an eye on it, and me. He didn't have to. Lieutenant Davis had been my watch commander as long as I was a beat officer. When a sudden flurry of murders overwhelmed the three-man Homicide Detail, it was Lieutenant Davis who recommended me for the assignment. Lieutenant Davis, black, with a master's degree, would be a candidate when the captain's job opened up. He was a stickler for thoroughness and detail—he had caught plenty of my mistakes over the years. But he'd also insisted I go to Homicide School, the two-week investigation classes offered by the state. And he'd given me his stamp of approval for the promotion. His prestige was on the line, almost as much as mine.

"I'd like to stay on the case, Lieutenant," Pereira said.

He nodded. It was a beat officer's right to request being kept on the team that handled what had originally been her case.

"And it's still mine till the transfer, right?" Pereira asked.

There was no need for an answer.

"Then I'll take one of my few opportunities to assign someone else duties. Are you still offering help, Jill?"

"Might as well."

"Okay, how about seeing the widow?"

It was a moment before I said, "Yes, of course."

When the others had left—Lieutenant Davis to start his car and head back to the station or home (his shift had officially ended over an hour ago) and Misco for another engagement under the tarp—Pereira said in a low voice, "Thanks, I really hate seeing the families."

"I'd have to see her later anyway. It'll be easier on her to deal with just one of us."

"Still, thanks."

"Let me check the contents of the car before I go."

"Sure." She led me to the Cadillac's trunk and opened it. It was huge (it looked big enough to put my car in) and empty but for a jack. "Spare's in place. Carpet looks clean. Lab guys have been over it. Even Misco figured there was nothing out of sorts here. The rest of the stuff from inside the car is in bags in the squad car."

I followed her across the circle, automatically looking down for skid marks, for a moment forgetting that the Cadillac hadn't skidded but bounced across the roadway to the cement fence. Pereira pulled open the passenger door of her car. She held up a plastic bag filled with cigarette ash. "From the ashtrays in the back." One other small bag held ash from the front passenger's tray.

"How about the driver's?"

"Empty," she said. "There was nothing on the seat. Ordinary dirt and pebbles on the floor." She indicated a third bag. "Ordinary stuff in the glove compartment."

The glove compartment bag was considerably fuller. I went through it carefully, noting maps of Berkeley and San Francisco, a pack of tissues, an unopened flashlight pen, a service record from Trent Cadillac in Berkeley. I pulled out a yellow copy of the report from today's work.

"Misco says it's the standard servicing—you know, the six-thousand-mile checkup."

I nodded hesitantly.

Pereira smiled. "People with new cars, Jill, take them in every six thousand miles, so they don't end up like yours."

"Okay, okay. So the driver, Palmerston, took his car to be serviced today, had it checked over completely, and" —I noted the bottom of the form—"signed 'approved by

Sam N-something' at one-thirty. So at one-thirty this car should have been in perfect condition, right?"

"Right. And according to Misco the mechanic there is tops."

I replaced the form and pulled out the remaining paper. Holding it closer to the light over the door, I made out the handwriting. " 'Shareholders Five,' and there's a phone number. Any ideas on that?"

"Nothing."

"Palmerston's writing?"

"Could be. The ink could be from the pen in the glove compartment. Color looks the same."

Putting it back, I said, "Have the print guys do it right away."

"I'll tell them. Whether they get to it today is another thing."

"What about the deceased's pockets?"

"Just a wallet. Not even a handkerchief."

I pulled the wallet from its bag. It held six twenties, Visa, American Express, and Diner's Club cards, and a driver's license that indicated Palmerston had been sixty years old, five foot ten, 155 pounds, and needed glasses to drive. I held his picture closer to the light. Driver's license photos rarely capture the spirit of the driver. Most people look angry or foolish with fright. The lighting is bad, the process haphazard. But Ralph Palmerston had been lucky. His blue eyes were clear and bright, his white hair thick, wavy, and the lines of his chiseled nose clear. His smile looked genuine. He looked like a nice man, like a man who shouldn't have ended his life with blood and terror in his eyes.

"All this doesn't tell me much," I said, handing Pereira the wallet. "I'll feel better when I know more about Palmerston."

"You should feel better now then. Ralph Benedict Palmerston was one of the scions of the Berkeley mon-eyed establishment."

I stared. Pereira's theoretical knowledge of finance was well known in the department and her fascination with the San Francisco money scene unmatched. "I didn't know Berkeley had a moneyed establishment."

"All of Berkeley isn't propped against the wall on Telegraph Avenue begging for spare change."

"Still, even people who have money are too 'Berkeley' to become 'establishment.' If they're interested in that scene, they move to Pacific Heights."

Pereira nodded. Rain dripped from her short blond hair. "I don't know why Palmerston stayed in Berkeley. But he has been part of the wealthy in-group for years. You know—Chamber of Commerce, charities. He's well known for his charity work. Until the last few years he spent most of his time that way—chairman of this fund-raising dinner or that campaign. I know for a fact that he spearheaded a drive for aid to a Vietnamese refugee camp that netted over a million dollars—big time for a local effort."

"Where does his money come from?"

"Palmieri Winery. He's an heir."

"Doesn't he have to work there?"

"No. It's pretty common knowledge that Palmerston's father, who was one of two brothers, had no interest in the business. He gave his voting rights to his brother in return for a guarantee of fifty-five percent of the profits."

"That hardly sounds fair. The brother does all the work and Palmerston's father collects the lion's share of the money."

Pereira shrugged. "The story is that the brother loved the winery and would have given anything for total control. As far as I know, he never complained."

"And now? What about his children? Do they still run the winery and give Palmerston fifty-five percent?"

"There aren't any children. There were two sons but both are dead—no heirs. So the brother's share of the winery went to a corporation with the same clause about

Palmerston's percentage. As I remember, it's a big corporation, too big to kill for the Palmieri net profits, if that's what you're thinking."

It was exactly what had crossed my mind.

"He looked like a nice man," I said.

"Everything I've heard suggests that he was."

"I wonder why he stopped working with charity the last few years."

"He got married."

"And?"

"Wait till you see his wife."

3

From the traffic circle, I looked up Marin Avenue. It was as steep as any street in San Francisco. On the night of the first rain, when the oil drippings from the long dry season were still on the pavement, any road would be slick. For a sixty-year-old man with bad eyesight, driving down the steepest street in town at dusk would be challenge enough. When his brakes failed, he wouldn't have a chance.

I started my Volkswagen and headed up the milder incline of Los Angeles Avenue. From there I tacked back and forth along the hillside streets, taking a path that I had perfected during the three years since my car had died halfway up Marin and I'd had to roll back down to the intersection. My new path was good, but it did take twice as long to get to Grizzly Peak Boulevard at the top.

The Berkeley hills are not really individual hills but part of a ridge created when the earth's plates slammed together at the Hayward Fault. The hills run from Contra Costa County to the north, through Berkeley, Oakland, Hayward, and Fremont, the towns to the south. Houses jostle for space from the Berkeley flatlands up the hillside to Grizzly Peak. Between Grizzly Peak and the wilderness of Tilden Park to the east are a few streets and cul-de-sacs of homes with views that jack their selling prices up toward half a million dollars. Ralph Palmerston's was one of these. It was a pale stucco Spanish style built around three sides of a twenty-five-foot-square courtyard, with the living room to the left, the garage to the right, and a bougainvillea-covered courtyard wall connecting them. The wall was five feet high, with decorative iron spikes atop it. It couldn't be climbed unobtrusively.

I pulled up in front and walked to the gate. It was locked. I pushed the bell and waited, anxious to see Ralph Palmerston's wife—the woman whose arrival had stopped his charitable impulses—dreading the moment when I would have to tell her about his death. The picture of Ralph Palmerston lying there with the pulser lights blinking on his face came to my mind. I swallowed and stared hard at the courtyard wall, reminding myself that I was a Homicide detective now. My job was dead bodies. I would see plenty worse-looking than Ralph Palmerston's, with its terror-stricken face. There would be times I'd see corpses without anything left of their faces at all.

The house was dark. Even with the streetlight shining on the picture window in the living room, I couldn't make out what was inside. There were interior shutters; the lower ones were closed. But I did spot the wires of a security system.

As I rang the bell again, I thought that Ralph Palmerston was too careful a man to leave his house dark. His accident had been at four thirty-eight. Now at six, dusk was turning to dark. It was the time that a careful man would have the lights on and all the shutters closed. So wherever he had been going, Ralph Palmerston would have planned to be home before now.

I knocked a third time, but it was becoming clear that no one was going to answer.

I checked with the neighbors on either side, but neither knew where Mrs. Palmerston was. I had told Pereira I would notify the widow. I could wait or come back. I chose the latter.

Knowing Misco, he would be at the dealership where Palmerston's car had been serviced. He'd be talking to the mechanic.

I climbed into my car and headed for the flatlands.

Trent Cadillac, showroom and shop, was on Shattuck Avenue, one of Berkeley's main north-south streets. It was in the automobile ghetto, where a prospective buyer could check out Isuzus, Subarus, Hondas, Peugeots, Volvos, Nissans, and assorted domestic vehicles without leaving the street. The Honda and Volvo showrooms were dark. Doubtless their salesmen didn't need to spend their evening hours at work; they had ample time during the day to tell customers they could put their names on their waiting lists.

Fortunately for me, Trent Cadillac's employees didn't share their presumptions. I pulled up in front of the showroom, and raced for the door. Even in those few steps I got soaked again. I stopped inside and shook my head vigorously. When I looked up, I noticed the salesman, a tall sandy-haired man, leaning back in his chair, laughing. Even though he was laughing at me, I couldn't help noticing how attractive he was.

"Sorry," I said.

"It's okay. Anything to bring customers in." He stood up languidly and ambled toward me. He wore a tan jacket and light pants, both just a mite too large. On him they looked not ill-fitting, but comfortable. He had that air of moneyed sureness that made whatever he wore de rigueur. As he came up to me, he glanced out the door at my battered Volkswagen. "Are you thinking of trading up?"

I laughed. "I'm with the police department. Actually, I'm just cutting through here on my way to the shop. One of our Traffic Investigators is probably still there.

Besides, it looks suspicious for a police officer to drive a Cadillac."

He shrugged, as if to say some officers could carry it off. "I'll take you back there."

"I don't want to keep you from your post."

"No problem. Not tonight. A huge thunderstorm doesn't incite people to buy Cadillacs." His hand brushed my shoulder as he headed me between the highly polished limousines. "You might consider the advantages of conducting your interviews in this model," he said, indicating a huge silver vehicle with a bar and television in back.

"Or barring that, I could just move in."

It was a moment before he smiled, a moment that said he was forcing a polite response to an unamusing comment. He looked like William Powell in a Thin Man movie: repartee was all important, and I had made a remark that hadn't measured up.

"There he is," I said, spotting Misco. In contrast to the salesman, Misco suddenly seemed small, dark, and frenetic, and very comfortable. "Thanks for your help," I said to the salesman.

He caught my eye, smiled, and ambled off, like William Powell heading for another drink. I turned to Misco. He was standing near the rear exit with the mechanic, an Asian of about thirty-five or forty.

Indicating him, Misco said to me, "Sam did the work on the Palmerston car. The car was right where we are now. Checked out, huh, Sam?"

The mechanic extended a wiped hand. "Sam Nguyen," he said with something of an accent. "I have told your colleague that I have completed all essential adjustments on the Palmerston vehicle. I have changed oil personally and lubed. Palmerston vehicle is A-1."

"You checked the brakes?"

"I checked brakes, of course. I examined whole car." His voice was rising. "I am not what you call a trainee.

Sam Nguyen did not become a mechanic here on a government refugee program."

I nodded.

"I am a mechanic. I was a mechanic in Saigon. There Sam Nguyen was esteemed. Everyone with a limousine came to Sam Nguyen. Many mechanics worked for me. I had a villa by the river, many servants." A smile of recollection flashed across his face. "They said, the powerful men who owned limousines, 'There is nothing Sam Nguyen cannot do.' I make a car that was bombed run again. I make customized job: bulletproof glass, no problem; folding bed, no problem; secret cargo space, no problem; machine gun—"

"I'm sure, Mr. Nguyen. But you're saying Mr. Palmerston's car was in perfect condition when it left here?"

"That is correct."

"Do you know when that was?"

"One-thirty, pronto. Mr. Palmerston is very particular about his car being waiting at that time."

"Do you know why?"

He looked at me oddly for a moment, as if I had asked a ridiculous question, then his face sank back into a noncommittal expression. "It is no problem. It does not take longer. I finished at one o'clock."

"You signed the work order. So at that time you guaranteed the brake lines were in good shape?"

His dark brows pushed together. "The brake lines were okay. I inspected them this morning."

"Could they have been faulty?"

"Holes large enough to let fluid through? Never. I, Sam Nguyen, checked the lines before okaying them. In Saigon, I go over everything looking for danger. Those holes would not escape Sam Nguyen."

"Thank you," I said.

Misco walked with me to the door. "I guess this case will be yours by tomorrow, huh, Smith?"

"Yes."

"Well, what I came out here to tell you was that Sam Nguyen is on the up-and-up. He really is a genius with cars. Trent Cadillac is lucky to have him. He's known all over the area, not just in Berkeley. Over there, in Saigon, they didn't have spare parts. When a manifold went, that was it, unless they could get the car to Sam's. Word is there's nothing he couldn't repair, replace, or improve on. The joke is that he revamped a Citroen into a villa."

"Loses something in the translation."

"Yeah, well . . . in a couple years this could be Nguyen Cadillac. Or maybe Nguyen Motors will be somewhere else. Sam doesn't just work on Caddies."

"So you believe him when he says the car was perfect when it left here?"

"Mechanically, he's the best."

"What about ethically? Could he be bought?"

"I don't know. But not about this. If Sam Nguyen had sabotaged Palmerston's car, we would never have found a clue."

I looked out at the rain. So Sam Nguyen finished the car at one o'clock. It was in perfect condition. Ralph Palmerston picked it up at one-thirty. And in three hours the brake lines were cut, the car smashed, and Ralph Palmerston was lying on the sidewalk with blood in his eyes.

I considered checking back at the station with Pereira and calling the phone number on the slip of paper in Palmerston's glove compartment, but I hated to think of Mrs. Palmerston pacing her living room wondering where her husband was. And I was getting more anxious and more curious to see this woman.

I made my way back via my circuitous route to Grizzly Peak Boulevard.

But Mrs. Palmerston was not worrying, or at least she wasn't doing it at home. The house was still dark.

There were lights now in most of the neighbors' houses. I started with one diagonally across the street.

The householder, a woman in her fifties, hadn't been home all day. She couldn't tell me anything. She looked at me suspiciously. Again, I wished I had had the sense to bring an umbrella to work. It was no wonder a bedraggled, sodden woman claiming to be a Homicide officer engendered skepticism.

The man to the right of her house had just returned from work. He didn't know the Palmerstons; he'd only lived there eight months.

It wasn't till I knocked on the door of the house across the street that I was rewarded.

The woman who answered the door—Ellen Kershon was her name—was not much older than I was, probably in her early thirties. But in contrast to me, she had styled hair—dry—and wore a soft corduroy knickers outfit. The leather of her boots looked softer than the corduroy.

"I'm Detective Smith," I said, holding out my shield. "It's about your neighbor Ralph Palmerston. He's been in an accident."

She shrunk back. "An accident? Is he all right?"

"I'm afraid not. He's been killed."

Tears welled in her eyes. "But how?"

"His car crashed into the guardrail in the Marin traffic circle." I didn't elaborate; I'd already told her more than I should have before the widow was notified.

She covered her face, and in that moment she looked more like a child in knickers than an adult. Swallowing, she motioned me into the living room, a large comfortable room with thick green wall-to-wall carpeting. By the front window was a jack-o'-lantern.

"I'm sorry," she said, swallowing again. "I don't usually react like this."

"Were you very close to Mr. Palmerston?"

"Actually no, that's the strange thing. I wouldn't have thought his death would affect me so much. Sit down." She settled on a maroon sofa and I followed. "I grew up in this house. Ralph was really a friend of my parents, a rather formal friend. They went to his Christmas open house, and he came here for my parents' annual barbecue. Ralph didn't have children. When I was a small child, Ralph's wife was frail; later on she drifted into more serious illness. Eventually she died. Ralph was devoted to her. She took a lot of his time. Maybe that's why he seemed so formal."

So far her explanation hadn't explained her reaction. I waited.

"He was a thoughtful man. Every Christmas he gave my parents a case of champagne, the winery's private reserve—I mean their private private reserve, not the so-called private reserve you see in stores. And to me"—her eyes clouded—"his gifts were always the perfect thing. Each year it was something very special—a basketball and hoop when I was thirteen and thought I'd never lower myself to be interested in boys, and French perfume the next year when I was going on my first date. Always just the right thing. It wasn't till I had my own child that I wondered how he could have zeroed in on what I wouldn't have known I'd adore. Surprising for a man who never had children."

I nodded. The aroma of beef filled the living room. It reminded me that I had been headed for ice cream an hour and a half ago.

"In a way, I'm not surprised," she said slowly, "about the accident, I mean. It was such a shame. All those years with his first wife so sickly. He had his health but he couldn't go anywhere. And then in the last six months his own eyesight started to go. He's hardly driven at all in the last two months. He didn't want to endanger people."

"But he did drive today."

"Today he almost hit Billy." The words seemed to burst out, as if Palmerston's prior thoughtfulness made this offense that much worse.

"Billy's your son?"

"What? Oh, yes."

"Is he here?'

"He's in his room."

"Can I talk to him?'

She nodded and opened a door to a staircase. "Billy," she called. "Put your robe on and come down. There's a police officer here who wants to talk to you about Mr. Palmerston." To me, she added, "He's in bed, trying to avoid catching pneumonia."

But when Billy ambled down the stairs, he was wearing jeans and a sweater. He was a long-blond-haired adolescent who clearly had had a large spurt of growth and had not filled out to match it yet. He looked like a vision in a tall, thin mirror.

"You weren't in bed, were you?" his mother demanded.

"Aw, Ma . . ."

To me, she said, "He rode his bike to school this morning. Of course it was pouring when school was out. I went to pick him up. We could have put the bike in the back of the wagon. We've done it plenty of times before, right, Billy?" she demanded, turning to him.

"Aw, Ma . . ."

"But no, when I got to school he was gone. He had to ride his bike to the top of the hills so he could see the storm better. Can you believe that?"

"She doesn't look so dry herself," Billy put in.

"Billy!"

"Your mother says you saw Mr. Palmerston today," I said to him.

"He nearly creamed me! Jeez, he came this close." He held his hands inches apart.

"How close?"

"Well, maybe this far." Now it was a foot. "But it was close. He didn't even see me."

"Where were you?"

"In the street. I was just making my cut for the driveway. See, if you stay on the other side of the street till you're right across from the driveway, there's this bump. You can hit it and bounce and then the edge of the driveway gives you another bounce."

Billy's mother sighed. "Two thousand dollars on orthodontia . . ."

"Where were you and where was he?"

"I was making my cut. He was up the street, driving real slow like he always did. He's old. But then he started to turn for his garage and he speeded up. He barely missed me."

"When was that?"

"I don't know."

"I know, exactly," Mrs. Kershon said. "It was one fifty-three. Billy got out of school early today. There was a teachers' meeting. I'd been watching for him since one-thirty. I was sure he'd been hit by lightning. Instead, he was off seeing how wet he could get."

Before Billy could get out his "Aw, Ma," I said, "You said Mr. Palmerston hadn't driven in two months, but today he picked up his car from the repair shop and went out with it this afternoon. Do you have any idea where he was going?"

"No," she said slowly. "When they go out, his new wife drives him. They take her car. I'm surprised his needed to be serviced, he used it so rarely."

Billy opened his mouth and then let it close.

"Do you have any idea where Mrs. Palmerston is now?"

"No. She doesn't go out all that much without him."

Billy squirmed forward on his chair.

"Sit still," his mother snapped. To me, she said, "They never leave the lights out. We've had burglaries. You must know that. Ralph has always been very careful. He has some lovely pieces and it would be a pity to have them stolen."

I nodded, recalling my similar reaction to their darkened windows. "Mrs. Kershon, I understand that Mr.

Palmerston used to be very active in charity work, but has stopped that in the last few years. . . ." I let the thought hang.

"Since he married Lois," she said, picking it up.

"Why do you think he changed?"

Mrs. Kershon fingered her soft blond hair. She glanced at Billy as if assessing whether to speak in front of him.

But it was Billy who spoke. "She's got more important stuff to spend money on than charity."

"Billy!"

"It's true, Ma. She's got a Mercedes. She's got fur coats. Boy, I sure haven't seen her putting a quarter in the Free Clinic box."

Mrs. Kershon started to speak to him again, then caught herself and shrugged. "It's true, Officer. I don't know her well—hardly at all, but she doesn't look . . . well, she looks like she devotes most of her thoughts to her appearance. You know what I mean."

I did, but I said, "Can you give me any examples?"

"Examples? She looks like a model. And she's a lot younger than Ralph."

Picking up the unspoken inference, I asked, "Do you think she married him for his money?"

"Well, I don't want to make judgments, I mean, I hardly know the woman, so I really can't say what her motivations were."

"That's not what you said to Dad."

"Billy!"

I stared at her, fighting to control a grin. "Mrs. Kershon?"

"Well, okay, off the record, I can't think what else would have motivated Lois. She's very attractive, very sure of herself. Ralph is a nice man. He would make some woman a lovely husband. But not Lois Palmerston." She paused. "The thing is, Officer, Lois Palmerston doesn't look like a woman for whom *nice* would be enough, if you know what I mean."

Billy was sitting on the edge of his chair, his knees tapping together.

"Well, thank you, Mrs. Kershon." I gave her my card, with the old extension crossed out and my new Homicide one inked in. "You'll let me know if you hear anything, won't you?"

"Of course."

I stood up and started for the door. "One more thing. As long as Billy is dressed anyway, I wonder if he could show me the exact spot in the street where Ralph Palmerston nearly hit him. We'll use an umbrella."

"Sure," she said. "He's either going to get pneumonia or not now. But you put your jacket on, Billy."

Without pause he headed to a closet and drew out a jacket and umbrella.

Once outside, I said, "What did you want to tell me?"

"Gee, how did you know—"

"Police training," I said with a straight face.

"See, I couldn't tell you in front of my mother. I mean, she sent me to bed, right after I got home. Like I was a baby. She'd kill me if she knew I'd gone back outside, I mean, after she told me to stay in bed." Suddenly he looked frightened. "You won't tell, will you?"

"Not unless it's vital to the case. And if that happens there'll be so much going on that it won't matter." I waited till he nodded, then said, "So you went back outside."

"See, I really wanted to see the lightning and all. I figured I'd ride my bike up into Tilden Park and find a spot under the trees and watch."

"What *did* you do?" We were standing in the middle of the street. The wind was tossing the rain against our legs; rain bounced off the macadam onto our ankles.

"Well, I got my bike and I started out into the street and then Mr. Palmerston backed out of his garage. He nearly hit me."

"You said he nearly hit you when you were coming home from school."

"Well, he came close then, but this was the time he nearly hit me. Of course, I didn't tell Mom that. I started telling her about him nearly hitting me and I was telling her before I realized that I'd better not. So I adjusted things quick."

"And?" I hoped this wasn't all I was standing here in the rain to learn.

"Well, he stopped. He felt real bad. But he said he was in a big hurry. He was going for his wife. It was an emergency."

"Did he say where she was?"

"Yeah. That's the really interesting part." Billy stared straight at me, enjoying his moment of suspense. "He said they called and told him to come and get her out. She was at the Albany Police Department."

4

I had Billy Kershon repeat exactly what he recalled
Ralph Palmerston telling him: "They called and said my
wife was being held at the Albany Police Department. I
have to go and get her." He wasn't sure whether he had
said "get her" or "get her out." He didn't know why she
was there. He didn't think Ralph Palmerston did either.
What he did think was that Ralph Palmerston was as
frantic as he'd ever seen him.

Whatever Mrs. Palmerston was doing there, her presence at the Albany Police Department explained why
Ralph Palmerston, who hesitated to drive because of his
eyesight, ventured out on the stormiest night of the year
and drove down the steepest street in town. Marin Avenue led directly to the police station.

I considered going back inside the Kershon house and
asking to use the phone privately, but decided against it. I
would have to go and get Mrs. Palmerston anyway. So I
drove down, around the Marin traffic circle, which was
now free of any evidence of Ralph Palmerston's accident,
except for the bent metal divider. Cars moved cautiously,
lights bright, windshield wipers on high. From there
down Marin Avenue to the bay it was less steep—just a
normally sloping street. Huge trees formed a canopy over
the pavement along the Berkeley portion of the avenue.
Past the Albany line the tops were lopped off to accom-

modate the power lines. I drove one mile to the police station and pulled into their lot.

It took me only five minutes to discover that they had no Palmerstons in custody, none who had been in custody, and indeed, no record of a Ralph or Lois Palmerston at all.

"So Palmerston picked up his car at one-thirty and drove directly home. Then about four-thirty or so, just when commuter traffic was starting to get heavy, someone called him and told him to come get his wife at the Albany Police Station," Pereira repeated. She was sitting at her desk in our own station squad room. Theoretically, now at nearly 9 P.M. it was not her desk, but the property of the night watch officer. But he was out on beat. Pereira had notes spread over the desk blotter. Her normally curled short blond hair hung limp from the rain. Frown lines were deep in her forehead, but her brown eyes were bright. The uneasy mix of intensity and exhaustion was clear on her face. This was her first murder case as a beat officer. Before the reorganization, she would have been in charge. Then beat officers handled anything on their beats, from jaywalking to murder. Now she could only request to be part of the investigation team, *my* investigation team. But I knew from my own experience on beat that once you've been in charge of a case, to you it never ceases being yours. "So someone made sure Ralph Palmerston would drive down that hill in the rain, someone who knew his brakes wouldn't take that kind of stress."

"And someone who didn't care if he smashed into three or four cars in the process of killing himself."

Pereira sat back in her chair. "What do we know about Palmerston? There's nothing on the Alpha file except that he owns a Cadillac. I'm checking with the Corpus file to see if he's been booked on anything anywhere else in the county, but I'm not hopeful."

I leaned back against the desk in front of her. "The

question of the moment is, where is Lois Palmerston? She's not at home. She's not at the Albany Police Station. Where is she?"

"Probably at the movies, Jill. After all, it's only nine o'clock. If this were any other night it wouldn't be strange for a woman to be away from home at nine. I mean she wasn't planning on her husband being killed."

"Maybe not."

She stared up at me. "What do you mean?"

"Palmerston's car was in perfect running order when he left the garage. He drove it directly home. Two hours or so later there were perforations in his brake lines. No one was there but him and his wife. He didn't cut those brake lines himself." I took a breath. "And then there's this note from the car's glove compartment—'Shareholders Five' and a phone number." Without much hope I picked up Pereira's phone and dialed. It rang ten times before I put it down. "Damn."

"It is nine o'clock, Jill. Lots of businesspeople go home before nine, particularly if they deal with the stock exchange. 'Shareholders Five' sounds like stocks. Those people have to be up at six in the morning to get the ticker tape from New York."

"I know, I know. I'd just like someone who has some information about this case to be around when I need to see them. Here." I passed her the paper. "See what you can find out about the phone number—whose it is—and anything about Shareholders Five."

"You know, Jill," Connie said, smiling, "it may be that I *can* find out about Shareholders Five. There's this guy, Paul Lucas, who keeps asking me out. He's not real attractive, but he's the most incredible font of financial gossip. He does financial planning in the city and he has to keep up on it. Honestly, Jill, going out with him is like watching a soap opera. You wouldn't believe what's going on in the upper echelons of Bechtel."

"Do you think he'd know anything about Ralph Palmerston?'

"He'll be embarrassed if he doesn't."

"And Shareholders Five?" I could feel my enthusiasm returning.

"He should. If there's informed opinion to be had, Paul will have it."

"You look like you could use a drink. Maybe you should give Paul a call. In the meantime I'll go back to the house and wait for Lois Palmerston to come home."

Connie sighed. "Gee, it's wonderful to be in charge, however briefly. I want to cherish this moment—someone else is going to be sitting in a cold car in the rain waiting for a widow while I'm heading for a brandy and soda."

"Don't worry, things will even out tomorrow."

The rain slashed against the high windows in the squad room as I walked through the corridor back to detective division to check my desk. There was nothing new on it; I didn't expect there would be. Actually there was barely anything on it at all, since I had only been assisting the regular guys with their cases so far. There were no messages in my IN box. The rain hitting the windows seemed louder. My car was three blocks away. I glanced at Howard's IN box. It held three slips of paper. After seeing Ralph Palmerston's body, this wager of Howard's and mine seemed almost obscenely trivial. I had mixed feelings about it in any case. I didn't want to beat Howard at anything right now. But not giving this my best would be condescending. Even if he never found out, I would know. And as for comparing it with the fact of Palmerston's murder, I knew that if I were to have a passably normal life, I couldn't let the auras of the deaths I investigated cover every other facet of my time.

I sighed, listening to the rain. Balancing my philosophical hesitation was the fact that this was the only way I would ever get a parking spot less than a quarter of a

mile from the station. If Howard's costume was as hard
to guess as he seemed to think, he must have bought it
somewhere. I couldn't see Howard at home, needle in
hand, stitching it up. And I couldn't see him giving his
home number to his couturier. Howard lived in a large
brown shingle house with five other guys. Leaving a message there was like tossing pennies into a fountain in
hopes your wish would be granted. No, if the secret cos-
tumer called Howard, it would be here. I picked up his
messages.

Two, I recognized as drug informants. The third was
his dentist. So much for covert investigation.

I would have liked to have sent a uniformed officer up
to watch the Palmerston house, but there was no chance
of the watch commander releasing anyone from traffic
tonight. By now those people who had stopped for a few
drinks after work, planning to wait out the storm, would
be giving up and stumbling to their cars to drive home.
The ambulances would be busier than ever.

What I wanted to do was go home and change into dry
clothes and eat. I thought fondly of the ice cream I'd
been headed for hours ago.

Instead, I hurried back to my car. The rain had eased a
bit now. Keeping under the trees I managed to get not
too much wetter than I already was. I had dried out a bit
in the station, so that I was mostly just squishy damp.

I followed my roundabout route back up to Grizzly
Peak. Even though Lois Palmerston had not been home,
I didn't really think she was on the run. There was no
reason for that. If she had *shot* her husband, then she
might be trying to vanish. But if she were responsible for
the damage to his brake lines, she had tried to make his
death look like an accident. A woman doesn't leave town
because her husband was killed in an auto accident. She
sits home and inherits.

So innocent or guilty, she should be returning home. I
hoped it would be soon.

It was. I hadn't been outside the house more than fifteen minutes when a Mercedes convertible pulled up to the garage. The door opened automatically. The Mercedes pulled to the left-hand side of the garage, next to the house, and in.

I waited till the light went on inside the house, then rang the bell.

Lois Palmerston was about five-nine, slender, with reddish blond hair pulled back above her ears and caught with tortoise shell combs. She had hazel eyes that seemed to pick up the color from her hair. The slight arch to her nose gave her otherwise model-like face character. She was still wearing a gray raincoat with a rust scarf inside the collar. She looked like she had just come from a fashion show. She looked like someone who always looked like that.

"Mrs. Palmerston, I'm Detective Smith, Berkeley Police Department. May I come in?"

"Yes," she said with the normal questioning hesitancy. She led me from the foyer into a large Spanish-style living room. She sat on one of the three sofas that, with the open hearth, formed the four sides of a square. Beyond one was a grand piano and several chairs, and beyond them a picture window, which I guessed would give the Palmerstons a view over the descending Berkeley hills into the flatlands, San Francisco Bay, and the Golden Gate Bridge. Tonight it showed only rain.

It would be no kindness to draw out what I had to tell her. Sitting beside her, I said, "I'm afraid I have bad news. Your husband has been in an accident. He's been killed."

Her reaction—surprise, disbelief, tears—was completely normal. Her questions—when had the accident happened, where—were what one expected.

"I understand he picked up his Cadillac at the dealer's around one-thirty and drove it straight home," I said.

"Yes. He got here just before two."

"Why did he pick up the car himself? I gather he didn't drive much of late."

She nodded. "Ralph had a degenerating eye condition. It's rare and the doctors weren't sure if even surgery could stop the progression. He was basically going blind. They thought perhaps an operation could help, but they didn't know and they didn't want to do anything at this stage. They planned to wait till after the new year. Ralph and I were leaving Saturday." A tear hung from her eye. "We were going to the Far East. Saturday we were flying to Tokyo. Ralph didn't want to sit at home and worry about going blind. He said if he was going to be blind, there was nothing he could do about it. He wanted to go and see things while he could. He said if worse came to worst, at least he'd have something to remember. We were going Saturday." Her voice broke. She grabbed for her purse and extricated a handkerchief.

I remembered Ralph Palmerston's expression. No wonder he had been terrified when his brakes failed. He probably couldn't even see the street in front of him.

"I'm all right now, Officer," she said, replacing the handkerchief and pulling out a pack of cigarettes.

"Why did your husband have his car serviced today? And why did he pick it up himself? Surely, if you couldn't get it, someone from the shop would have delivered it."

She lit a cigarette. "Why? Ralph's a very orderly man. He'd be uncomfortable leaving on a trip without everything being in order. I made plans to see a friend today because I knew Ralph was getting the car. He wouldn't mind my being gone." Her voice now was dispassionate, as if she were willing herself to look at Ralph and his death from a distance.

"But why did *he* pick it up?"

"He always took his car to be serviced. He always picked it up. It was what he did." She took a breath. "I doubt it even occurred to him not to pick it up. If he'd been asked to drive somewhere else, somewhere new, he would have decided it was unwise, but this, because it was something he had always done . . ."

"Is there no place else he would have driven?"

She considered the question, lightly tapping her teeth together. "I don't think he would. Ralph was a very responsible man." She looked directly at me. "But he did, didn't he? Where was he going?"

It was a rhetorical question. She didn't assume I would know the answer. The person who had called Ralph Palmerston and told him Lois was at the Albany Police Station wouldn't have expected him to tell anyone where he was going. They wouldn't have known he would nearly hit Billy Kershon and then stop to talk to him. I said, "Tell me what you did from the time he came home with the car."

She took a drag of the cigarette. "Well, I showered and dressed. Then Ralph and I had a glass of hot sake—it seemed so appropriate for such a rainy day—and we practiced our Japanese lessons for a while, probably forty-five minutes. Ralph wanted to be able to speak decently when we got to Japan. We realized early on that that was going to be an impossibility, but we kept trying. He said at least it would be fun to be able to say a few things in Japanese." That remembrance seemed to cut through her control; she took a final drag of the cigarette and crushed it out in the ashtray. "After that I had dinner plans with a friend."

"Can you give me her name and address?"

She hesitated a minute before saying, "Yes, of course. It's Carol Grogan. She lives on Ordway." But she didn't ask why I wanted to know.

"What time did you leave?"

"Ten to four. I remember, I looked."

Ordway was in Berkeley, a ten-minute drive from here. "Were you planning an early dinner?"

"Oh, the time, you mean? Well, she's a librarian and

this is her day off. Her children are in day care till five-thirty, so she asked me to come early and have a quiet drink before she had to go and pick them up. Dinner with two small boys is anything but calm."

I glanced down at her beige raw silk slacks. I was surprised they'd survived so well. She looked, in the pants and loose silk sweater, as if she'd been going to a cocktail party, hardly for a meal with children. "What did you do there?"

She looked at me questioningly. "We had a drink and talked. Then she picked up the boys."

"Didn't you go with her?"

"No."

"And then?"

"She came back with the boys and we had dinner."

"And?"

"She put the boys to bed and we talked a bit more and then I drove home. Look, why are you asking me this?"

"Because someone called your husband and told him you were being held at the Albany Police Station and he needed to come to get you."

"What?"

I repeated what I had told her.

"But why would anyone do that?"

I didn't mention the perforations in the brake lines. I wouldn't until Misco's report was in. "Somebody wanted your husband driving down Marin Avenue this afternoon in the rain."

"But why?"

"I don't know yet. Tell me about him."

She lit another cigarette. It was clear that the full implications of what I had told her hadn't sunk in yet. "We've been married four years."

"Where did you meet him?"

"At opening night at the opera. One of the parties. That was almost five years ago." She spoke quickly, nervously. "What do you want to know about him?"

"Did he have any business associates who would bene-
fit from his death?"

"No. His money came from the Palmieri Winery. He
was an heir, but he had no control; he just got the
money."

I recalled Pereira explaining that. "What happens to
his money now?"

"It comes to me."

"All of it?"

"All of it." There was at once a defiant hardness and a
rush of fear in her voice.

"I do need to see his will."

"Of course," she said more calmly. "I'll call Mr. Farrell, Ralph's lawyer, in the morning."

"Can you think of any enemies your husband had, or
people who might have had something against him?"

She took a drag of the cigarette and let the smoke out
slowly, her eyes half closed, as if in thought. "I really
can't, Officer. Ralph had no enemies. His business connections were superficial—Chamber of Commerce, things
like that."

"Chamber of Commerce?"

"The winery has a tasting room in Berkeley. The people who run the winery asked Ralph to represent them at
the Chamber. It was just for form's sake. And for Ralph
to keep in touch with some of the men he's met over the
years."

"Did he have any bad habits—drinking, or perhaps
gambling?"

"He drank socially, no more. Coming from a winery
family, he knew more about the dangers of alcohol than
most. He had an uncle who killed a woman driving
drunk. No, Ralph was very careful. As for gambling, our
money wasn't in stocks."

I couldn't help but think that the rich viewed gambling
rather differently than the police. "Could he have gam-

bled elsewhere? Reno? Vegas? The local racetracks? Football?"

Again she drew on the cigarette, pulling so deeply and intently that it looked as if she were about to suck the tobacco in through the filter. "I can't imagine that. We never went to the races, or watched sports. Ralph wouldn't have known enough about sports to make a bet. As for Reno, we've been there two or three times, but only to see the shows. Ralph never even played a slot machine."

"But he could have gambled without your knowing it," I insisted.

"Obviously," she snapped. "If you're going to ask me what I don't know, anything's possible."

"I mean," I said, making an effort to keep my voice neutral, "did he get calls that he didn't explain, or go off regularly, or transfer money frequently?"

"No. None of that."

"What about charities? He used to be known for his work with them."

"They wouldn't profit from his death. I won't be making a memorial bequest, if that's what you're thinking. Ralph gave them a lot of time and a lot of money."

"And then he stopped," I prompted.

"He became disillusioned with giving to people who don't appreciate it. You know, Officer, things need to be reciprocal to work. When you give a lot, you expect something back, not money, but appreciation, gratitude, something that says your effort wasn't just tossed down the hole. Ralph got tired of tossing himself away."

"Well, what did he do? With his time, I mean." That had come out sharper than I'd intended.

But Mrs. Palmerston didn't seem to notice my tone. She shrugged. "He didn't give up all charities. We still attended a number of functions—openings, dinners. We played bridge, traveled, he enjoyed the symphony, the ballet, the theater before his eyes got so bad. He gardened. There's a greenhouse out back. And then there was his photography, his darkroom downstairs, but of course, he hadn't done that lately."

"What about Shareholders Five?"

She crushed out the cigarette, then searched for the pack, extricated another, and lit it. "I don't know about that."

"Shareholders Five was a notation your husband had written down and put in his glove compartment. It was the only unusual thing there. It must have been important."

She took a long drag of the cigarette. "I don't have any idea." She started to take another drag, then said, "Ralph wanted to get everything in order before we left. He had the car serviced. He cataloged all the negatives he'd had in envelopes while he could still see to do it. And he was such a little boy in some ways. He got all caught up in Halloween. We must have ten pounds of chocolate in the kitchen. He said he wanted to see the children this year when they came to the door. He said he had some big surprise planned for Halloween, not just the chocolate, not just for the children."

"What did he mean?"

"He wouldn't tell me. He just said I'd be surprised."

Halloween was the day after tomorrow. I wondered if the surprise he had planned had led to his murder today.

5

I took Lois Palmerston to the morgue to identify the body. She was virtually silent on the drive there. I didn't say much either. My mind was on Ralph Palmerston as I had seen him lying by the roadside. It would be difficult enough for Lois to see him rolled out on the slab without having to see his face bloodied and horrified.

Perhaps she was thinking the same thing. She was under tight control when she walked into the viewing room. The room itself was enough to unnerve anyone. It was stainless steel, top to bottom, so that it could be hosed down. Ralph Palmerston's body, lying on a stainless-steel gurney, was covered with a plastic sheet that only made him look colder, grayer.

Lois kept her gaze on the floor until she was right next to the gurney. Then she looked up quickly, gasped, and turned away.

We walked slowly back to the car. I opened the passenger door for her and had to tell her to get in. But as soon as the car moved, she looked around nervously and started to talk. She seemed willing to discuss anything, to cover the remembrance of Ralph's body with a blanket of words. As I started up the hill, she said, "It'll be easier if you go up Spruce."

I smiled. "Not in this car. I tried a couple years ago."

Spruce, though not so steep as Marin, was a long incline. On it, it would just take longer for my car to die.

Lois looked puzzled. "Don't they give you cars?"

"There are a limited number. And with the rain, they'll all be in use."

She held the handle above the glove compartment; her feet were braced against the front. Friends who were used to other cars had been unnerved riding with me. It wasn't the smallness of the Volkswagen, but the slope of the hood that undid them. They looked through the windshield and saw not the protective hoods of their own cars, not a different hood, but nothing at all. "As if I'm about to drop off the end of the world," one had said.

"If I'd been thinking right," Lois said, "I would have driven. My car is in the garage."

Her Mercedes convertible; I remembered Billy Kershon mentioning that.

"Did your husband give it to you?" That sounded like the Ralph Palmerston that Ellen Kershon had told me about—the man who gave the perfect presents.

Lois's hand tightened on the grip above the glove compartment. "It was mine before we were married."

I turned right. "You must have had a good job, then."

"I was with Hammonds, in San Francisco."

"Oh, downtown?"

"Yes."

I tried to recall exactly what Hammonds did. The name was familiar. Dammit, Pereira would know. "Hammonds, are they a law firm?"

She almost laughed. There was a note of hysteria in that sound. "No. They're architects. They'd be appalled to be confused with lawyers."

I made another right-hand loop. "Were you an architect, then?"

"No, I was in customer relations." There had been a pause before she spoke. "Customer relations" sounded like a forced phrase.

We were getting close to Grizzly Peak. I let the car slow. "What did you do?"

She hesitated. Her hand was tighter on the handle. She seemed to be in a battle between avoiding the terrors of silence and talking about something she clearly wanted to keep to herself. "I did the usual things. I made the clients feel welcome. I helped them with their problems, arranged their appointments, took care of the small things that can make the difference in a working arrangement."

"Like a receptionist?"

"More than a receptionist," she snapped. She took a breath then said more calmly, "I did more than answer the phone."

I felt a pang of guilt in having pricked a sore spot right at this time. But she was, I reminded myself, a potential suspect. And she certainly was sensitive about having been a receptionist. Had Ralph Palmerston's friends remarked on that? Was "gold digger" not an unfamiliar term?

The house was only a couple of blocks away. I could ask about Ralph's friends' reaction to her, or one other question. There wasn't time for more.

"I'm sure you had a very responsible position. You'd need to, to afford a Mercedes." I waved a hand indicating my own car, though I had the feeling that after the trip up the hill, any further allusion to it was unnecessary.

"It was used."

"Even so . . ."

"A friend got it for me."

I waited.

"Actually he was the husband of a good friend. A woman I knew in college. She's really my closest friend."

"They must be close friends to get you a Mercedes."

"I don't mean he bought it. He found it for sale. It was going relatively cheaply. He's good with cars, so he could get the engine back in shape. And he could touch up the finish."

"That's a lot of work." I couldn't imagine what I would have had to do in order to get my ex-husband, much less anyone else's husband, to revamp a car for me.

Lois shrugged. In my peripheral vision the movement looked forced. "He likes working with cars, doing things with his hands."

I still found this level of altruism hard to believe. "What does he do otherwise?"

"Computers. He's started a small company, Munsonalysis. I don't know what they do, something technical." Her words were slower now, more controlled. "Jeffrey may have explained what they do. Computers are too abstract for me. He used to talk about them all the time. When they were married, he had computer stuff all over the house. It used to drive Nina crazy. He didn't want her to touch some of it. He said if she hit the wrong key, whole companies would erase. She could never remember which were the okay keys and which were the off-limits ones. So she never touched any of the machines. She had to watch her step all the time." Now she sounded more like she was talking to ward off my questions than from nervousness. But I couldn't be sure. But if she was hiding something, I didn't know what it was or what questions to ask. And sometimes these spontaneous chatterings of suspects, or potential suspects, were more revealing than their thought-out answers. So I let her go on.

"Nina's a poet—you know, Nina Munson?"

I nodded, though the name wasn't familiar to me.

"She's had some things published locally. She's really very good. She's not obsessed with house pride anymore." Lois smiled. "I guess she had enough of that."

"She and Jeffrey are divorced?"

"Irreconcilable differences. Real irreconcilable differences." She laughed nervously.

I waited.

"The end came when Jeffrey, in all seriousness, tried to teach Nina to use a computer. He'd tried for years, but on this last push he told her that a word processor would be wonderful for writing poetry on, because she could take out words or move them around. He said it was so easy to write with a word processor that he'd considered being a poet himself. But he decided there wasn't any money in it. Nina left him the next day."

I laughed too. We were in front of the house.

Turning to her, I said, "Are you sure your husband had no enemies? Even minor ones? Think a moment. Did he have any arguments, even ones that seemed insignificant to you?"

She sat, slowly releasing her hand from the handle above the glove compartment.

"Were there any friends he stopped seeing suddenly?"

"No. The only thing of this sort—it seems too silly to bring up at all—was this afternoon at the Cadillac dealership. Ralph was still angry when he got home. He thought they were brushing him aside. I remember, he said, "At least you expect courteous service when you're paying as much as that!"

"What exactly happened?"

"As clearly as I could piece things together, Ralph had paid for the car checkup and he was standing chatting with one of the salespeople when he saw the mechanic, that short Vietnamese—"

"Sam Nguyen?"

"Yes, Sam Nguyen. He was headed to the door at the back of the repair shop. Ralph called to him, but he didn't answer. He never bothered to turn around. He just walked out the door."

"Is that all?"

"Ralph was furious. Any other man might have figured the mechanic didn't hear, or was preoccupied. But Ralph had very set ideas about courtesy, particularly courtesy in business. He took the complaint to Jake Trent, the owner."

"And then what happened?"

"Nothing, according to Ralph. I guess Jake tried to smooth things over and Ralph wasn't having that. But, as Ralph said, Sam Nguyen could have kicked him in the teeth and Jake Trent wouldn't have done anything. He's too afraid of losing Nguyen."

I had hoped for something better.

Lois opened the car door. We hurried through the rain and wind to the door. I waited while she turned on the lights. I offered to stay awhile, but she clearly didn't want that. I suggested that she call a friend—Nina, or the woman with whom she'd had dinner, Carol Grogan. Her no was immediate. She was sure she'd be fine alone. She had sleeping tablets. What she needed was rest, she assured me, as she held the door open.

I ran back around the car, yanked open the driver's door, and flopped onto the seat before the wind blew the door shut.

Lois Palmerston had been understandably upset after seeing her husband in the morgue. But she had regained control surprisingly quickly. Was that ability to rebound an innate skill, or did it mean she hadn't been unprepared for what she saw there? It was too soon for me to guess. But her talk on the way home, what had that told me?

For one thing she was very sensitive about having been a receptionist. I wondered how much more than a receptionist she had been. "Receptionist" can be very legitimate, or it cannot. I wished now that I knew where Pereira was having her drink with the well-informed Paul Lucas. Hammonds was a prestigious firm in San Francisco. If Paul Lucas knew as much as Pereira thought, he might have heard if their receptionist was more than decorative.

And what of Lois Palmerston's friends? For someone who was willing at all costs to avoid silence on the drive home from the morgue, her instantaneous rejection of her friends as companions for this night was odd. Did she just want to avoid my staying around till one of them arrived? Another half an hour would have been difficult for her to fill with desultory conversation. Was there something in the house she didn't want me to see?

And Jeffrey, of Munsonalysis. What was his interest in Lois? He was divorced from her friend now. He had found and refurbished a Mercedes for Lois. Had he been more than merely the husband of a friend? Could he have left his wife for Lois, only to find her unwilling to divorce the wealthy Palmerston for a fledgling businessman who probably had more debts than cash? Lois had adjusted easily to the comforts money brought. I didn't see her abandoning them for passion. But as a widow, she could have both.

Tomorrow I would talk to Jeffrey. But tonight I could at least check up on Ralph Palmerston's brouhaha at Trent Cadillac.

When I got back to the station, I left instructions for Carol Grogan's beat officer to make a preliminary check on Lois Palmerston's alibi, then got out the phone book and dialed the home number for Jacob Trent. It was late to be calling a witness, but I wanted to talk to him before a night's sleep dulled his memory of Ralph Palmerston's outburst.

He answered on the fifth ring.

"Mr. Trent, this is Detective Smith, Berkeley Police."

"Is something the matter?"

"I'm investigating the death of Ralph Palmerston. He was in your repair shop this afternoon."

"Jesus. It's nearly eleven o'clock. What do you mean calling me at this hour?"

"Ralph Palmerston has been murdered."

There was a silence. "Murdered?"

"Yes."

"Well, what does that have to do with me? We just repaired his car. The guy hassled us as it is. Look, lady, I don't have enough trouble? I got Sam Nguyen, my best mechanic, wanting to go to Hong Kong for Chinese New Year. New Year's in February. Nguyen wants to leave in December. Two months, I ask you. Then I got a detective bugging me about one of the salesmen, and now you calling me about Palmerston. And Palmerston himself throwing his weight around."

"Exactly what happened to Mr. Palmerston today?"

"Lady, I have no idea. By the time I realized anything had happened, Palmerston was barging into my office, shouting for all the world to hear. I was on the phone—business—how do you think that sounded?"

"What did Mr. Palmerston *say* happened?"

"He was shouting that Sam Nguyen stalked off the floor when he wanted to talk to him."

"How do you know it was Sam Nguyen?"

"I saw him. Besides, he's a little Oriental, couldn't be more than five-two. The other mechanics are big, husky guys. They've got light hair. Is that enough difference for you?"

"What did Mr. Palmerston want to talk about?"

"He never said, and believe me, I didn't ask. Palmerston may not be in business himself, but he's got a lot of connections in the business community. He's done a lot of charity work. He knows people. He can call in favors. I didn't want to get on the wrong side of him. I'll tell you the truth, lady, if it was another customer, I wouldn't have taken the time I did to calm him down. If it was any other mechanic, I would have fired him."

"What shape was Mr. Palmerston in when he left?"

"He was okay. I let him talk about the proper respect for customers awhile. That calmed him down. He's an old-school guy; he expects business to be conducted with a certain grace. God knows how he's survived in Berkeley this long. I told him I'd pass on his message to Nguyen and have Nguyen get back to him."

"And did you?"

"He said not to bother."

Thanking him, I turned back to my notes. It wasn't till I came back from the dictating cubicle that I noticed the message in my IN box. It was from Pereira: *Surprise! I couldn't find out anything about Shareholders Five, but the phone number belongs to our old friend Herman Ott.*

6

Our old friend Herman Ott was about forty. He was blond and sallow-complected, with a short trunk, spindly legs, and a noticeable gut; and he perpetually wore a yellow sweater. He looked like a canary.

What Herman Ott was, was a private detective. He had begun his student days at Cal during the sixties. During those years he had gotten a job, part-time at first, with a detective too old to do his own legwork. He moved out of the dorm and rented two rooms in a shabby Telegraph Avenue building. Sometime later those rooms had metamorphosed into the office of the Ott Detective Agency. He'd never graduated. As the years went by, he took fewer and fewer classes. Presumably he would eventually accumulate enough credits for a degree, but I doubted it would matter. In many ways, Herman Ott still lived in the days of marijuana, Free Speech, antiwar demonstrations, and loathing of the Pigs.

It was after eleven when I finished the report. I should have gone home, if only to see how much water had dripped in through the jalousie windows that made up three walls of my porched-turned-studio apartment. Instead I turned east toward Telegraph. One advantage of dealing with a detective who lives in his office is he's likely to be there at night.

Telegraph Avenue leads directly off the campus. It is

the center of the students' commercial world. The head shops and Indian clothing stores that used to characterize it are giving way to boutiques and gelato shops, but the sidewalks are still filled with street artists. Students and former students still ponder their goods. And, seemingly unaware that the sixties ended over a decade ago, rag-covered addicts still wander the avenue or prop themselves against buildings and ask for spare change.

But for the most part, Telegraph Avenue closes down with the departure of the sun. At night the shops are dark, the sidewalks empty, and the yellow glow from the streetlights shines overbright against the emptiness of the sidewalks. The only pedestrians are students hurrying from night classes, or the occasional drug burnout still propped against a building. Even on the street itself you rarely see another car.

And now, at nearly midnight, the students were gone and the avenue looked like a set from a long-completed movie.

I left my car in a red zone in front of Ott's building and ran for the staircase that huddled darkly between a pizza take-out and a poster shop. I stood for a moment waiting for my eyes to adjust and wondering what regulation the landlord had broken in failing to provide an entryway light. But considering the condition of the building, that had to be the least of his infractions.

I made my way up the steps. The entry door was at the top. Not surprisingly, it was unlocked. Inside, the hall-way was warm, and the smell of stale marijuana filled the air. I followed the staircase around and up to the third floor.

A dim light shone through the frosted glass panel of Ott's office. It outlined the metal bars behind it. I knocked.

Ott wasn't likely to pay for electricity when he wasn't there. He was more likely to count on his reputation for coming out bruised but on top. He'd survived in this seedy establishment for nearly twenty years. Half of his clients were on drugs. In his early days another large slice of his clientele was so anti-establishment that they would have found not paying his bill laudable. But Ott had always made his rent, and as far as I knew he had never been hospitalized. And he had never given the police incriminating information about a client. He'd never cooperated with us unless there was something in it for him.

I pounded on the door. In my years on this beat I had tried to get information out of Ott four or five times, but succeeded only once, when it was clear to both of us that I could haul him in for obstructing justice.

Inside, I could hear a grunt.

I pounded harder.

"Okay, okay, keep your pants on."

Ott pulled open the door and stared at me through half-closed eyes. He looked like he was sleepwalking, but I knew his reputation better than to believe that. He was shorter than I, his limp blond hair thinning on top. A gold-and-brown flannel shirt was half in and half out of his tan cords. Behind him, flung over the back of his desk chair, I could see his familiar yellow sweater. He looked a bit plumper than I recalled, as if the canary were about to lay an egg.

"Well?" he demanded, staring at my face, puzzled. The other times he had seen me I had been in uniform.

"Police." I held out my shield.

He glanced at it and back to my face. "Oh, yeah, you."

I pocketed the shield and stepped forward.

He didn't move.

"You want to talk in the hall?" I asked, letting the edge to my voice match his.

He shrugged.

"It's your case we'll be talking about. If you want that broadcast through the building . . ."

Across the hall the sound of a television was lowered. The building was supposed to be commercial now, but probably ninety percent of the "offices" doubled as apartments. Some tenants didn't even bother with the pretense of work.

Ott stepped back and I followed him into the ten-by-twelve room. An old wooden desk dominated it. Behind that were two file cabinets and the leather desk chair that held the yellow sweater. There was a soot-coated window next to the files and a bookcase on the far side of it. Through the connecting doorway I could see the second room, with its unmade folding bed, a formerly overstuffed chair that was now understuffed, and clothes and blankets and books strewn on top of everything. But the office where we stood now looked as if it belonged to someone other than the sloven who slept next door. Here, every file on the desk was in order, messages were in a pile next to the phone, and pencils and pens were in a mug. It was the office of a man who could put his hands on anything he needed.

But it was not an office I pictured Ralph Palmerston in. "Ralph Palmerston is dead."

Herman Ott's eyelids flickered, then his face became immobile. "So?"

"We found a notation and your phone number in his glove compartment."

Still, he didn't move.

"I need to know what you were doing for him."

"Officer, I can't tell you that."

"Your client's dead, murdered. What you've found out for him will be evidence."

"You know I can't reveal—"

"I know you can. It's just a question of when. You don't *have* a client now. I can go through legal procedures. I can waste a lot of time. I'm serious about this. In case you've missed it, it's midnight, I'm soaking wet, and I'm not willing to wait around while you play hard to get."

"I'm within my rights."

"For the moment. There'll come a time, soon, that you'll be withholding evidence."

"I'll wait."

I leaned back against the doorjamb. He was still standing beside his massive desk. "Look, I know Palmerston was your client. He's not going to be coming back for your report; he's not going to care what you've told me."

His pale, narrow mouth hardened.

"And Ott, he's not going to pay you."

"His heirs—"

"I've talked to his heir. His heir doesn't know anything about this." His mouth opened slightly. I could see I'd gotten to him. "Now it's possible, Ott, that we'll use your information when we go to trial. It's possible that the DA will need some background on Palmerston's killer. He has to hire someone—"

"I don't work for the DA."

Damn. I should have remembered that. "We have a discretionary fund. We may need to buy some of your work. You can deal with us or not deal at all. No one else is going to want it."

His pale brown eyes were set deep. Now the lids half closed over them as he considered. "What are you offering?"

"Tell me what you have and I'll put in a request."

"Not good enough."

"You've got my word that I'll make the request for what your info's worth. It's the best you're going to get. I've only been on this case since this afternoon; it's not even officially a homicide yet. You wait another day, and I'll have a lead on this Shareholders Five from someone else."

He laughed. "Who else? The research is mine."

"The information is about someone, five someones. Given a few days I'll come across them. It just saves time for you to tell me."

He let the lids droop over his eyes again. I glanced at

the map of Berkeley on the wall beside his desk, at the phone directories stacked atop the file cabinets, at the smudged yellow sweater.

"Okay," he said, "but if you don't come through—"

"I'll come through. I know the rules as well as you do. Now what did Ralph Palmerston want?"

He leaned against the desk. "Palmerston made an appointment about a month ago. He asked me to check out some people."

"How many?"

He hesitated. "Five."

"Who were they?"

Again, he hesitated. "He only gave me one name."

"Why would he tell you to investigate five people and then give you the name of only one of them?"

"Maybe he wanted to see what I could find out before he committed any more money for the others." A hint of a smile showed on his tight mouth. "I'm not the type of businessman Palmerston is used to dealing with. He probably wanted to make sure I wouldn't take his money and run."

"Why *did* he come to you?"

"I'll give you my guess. I mean, I didn't ask him. If he wants to give me his business, and his money, who am I to complain? So what I figured was he chose someone he'd never run into anywhere else, someone he wouldn't have to worry about his lawyer hiring or his friends using for their divorces."

I glanced around the run-down office. Ott's assessment made sense. This was certainly not a place anyone else of Palmerston's standing would be likely to come.

"What was the name he did give you?"

"Officer—"

"Spare me, will you? Just the name."

His narrow lips pressed together. I could see that it was an effort for him to tell the police anything significant. "Adam Thede," he said.

"Adam Thede?"

"You said just the name."

"How long do you think it will take me to run a make on him? You could save me the trouble. Tell me what is common knowledge."

"He owns Sunny Sides Up, the natural foods breakfast place here on the avenue."

"What did Palmerston want to know about him?" Thede wouldn't serve wine, not at breakfast, not during the week, and most breakfast places on Telegraph were closed weekends.

"I'm going to tell you straight, Officer, exactly what Palmerston told me. He needed to know what was important to Thede. He said he wanted to do something for him, a surprise, and he wanted to know enough to make that surprise count."

"Were they friends, Palmerston and Thede?"

"Didn't say."

"Well, what did you find out?"

Ott looked down. For the first time I sensed the man was embarrassed. "Nothing Palmerston couldn't have discovered himself. Thede runs a high-quality health food breakfast place. He advertises that all his ingredients are fresh, that all are organically grown. Sunny Sides Up is his baby. So, I told Palmerston that his gift should be something connected with that."

"And what was it?"

"When are you putting in that request?"

"First thing in the morning."

He was about to protest.

"For Christ's sake, Ott, it's after midnight. The department's efficient, but we don't process vouchers in the middle of the night."

He nodded. "When I gave Palmerston my first report, he had me run a check on all Thede's suppliers to make sure they didn't smuggle in a bag of pesticide for their tomatoes or buy commercial lettuce and pass it off as organic."

"Were they on the up-and-up?"

"What do you think? Thede was probably making out better than most. About ninety percent were organic."

"So you told Palmerston that?"

"Gave him a list of suppliers, and a twenty-page report."

"I'll need a copy."

"You'll have to get it from him, his heirs, or whoever."

"Do you expect me to believe that you didn't keep a copy?"

Again, he looked embarrassed. Clearly, his business practices were as integral to him as Palmerston's standards of courtesy were to him. "Any other time you'd be right, but Palmerston insisted on both copies." He shrugged. "He paid."

"And the gift? What was he going to do with the information you got him?"

"I don't ask questions I don't get paid for."

He also didn't answer questions he didn't get paid for, and he made it clear that whatever I was requesting from the discretionary fund paid for what he had already told me, no more. Still, for dredging facts out of Herman Ott, this wasn't a bad showing.

I made my way down the dark staircase to my car. The streets were empty now, the rain lighter. In ten minutes I was pulling up in front of the Kepple house.

My apartment was in back. For close to fifty years it had been the back porch of the house until, in a flash of frugality, Mr. Kepple had seen a way to underwrite his retirement. With the addition of a few plumbing fixtures and a ten-by-forty strip of indoor-outdoor carpet, he had converted it into an apartment. Three walls were jalousie windows, the fourth the white aluminum siding that had been one of Mr. Kepple's earlier inspirations.

For me, after months of coming home to scathing arguments with Nat, now my ex-husband, moving into Mr. Kepple's creation was a perfect escape. It was so unorthodox, so unmarried. I put my clothes in the closet and my sleeping bag on the floor and called it home.

Pereira, who, with Howard, had heard all the ever-new outrages of my separation and divorce, had planned a house-warming party for me. She was waiting until I got settled, until the apartment was decorated. A year later, she was still waiting. I had bought a white wicker table and a chaise lounge, but the place still looked like a porch. Slowly, it had become clear that this was not because Nat had kept the sofa and coffee table. It was, as Pereira had said with a shudder, because this was a home suited to someone who drove my car.

I pulled the jalousied door open and turned on the light.

"Damn." Under all the windows, the rain had flowed in. The indoor-outdoor carpet looked like the bottom of a lily pond. It squished when I stepped on it.

I reached for the phone. Mr. Kepple had assured me that jalousie windows were as good in rain as plate glass. Perhaps. Perhaps ones that he hadn't installed himself would have been. But plate glass wouldn't have turned my apartment into a place more suited to otters than people.

I put down the phone. I was too tired to deal with Mr. Kepple tonight.

Picking up my sleeping bag, I carried it into the kitchen and spread it out on the floor.

I was just drifting off to sleep when I remembered that I'd never gotten the pint of ice cream I'd planned to have for dinner.

7

Seven-forty A.M. found me running to cross Martin Luther King Junior Way before the light turned red. Detectives' Morning Meeting was at seven forty-five. I didn't need my well-known reputation for tardiness to move up to Detective Division with me. The parking spot I'd managed to ace a Honda out of was two blocks east of King Way and one to the south, nearly at the Berkeley library.

As I rounded the corner near the station door, I almost smacked into Howard.

"Going out for track?" he asked.

After four blocks I was too breathless to answer. Howard, sauntering across from his garage, looked perfectly at ease.

When I regained my breath, I said, "I'm on my first murder case." Even to myself I sounded adolescently smug.

"Since when? I left with you yesterday and you didn't have a case then."

We walked in the main doors and headed up the stairs. "After I dropped you off, I was going to the ice cream shop—"

Howard shook his head. "Only you would be on your way for junk food and find a case." My proclivity for doughnuts, chocolate bars, and ice cream was also well known. "I assume you'll tell me about it after the meeting."

All of Detective Division was seated around the table. Howard and I slid into the remaining two chairs. The guys who had gotten there earlier had coffee from the machine; those who were really on top of things had thermoses. I envied both groups. Having forced myself up at quarter to seven, I hadn't had time for either.

The meeting was brief. The captain summarized the reports that had been on his desk, including mine, Pereira's from the scene of the crash (which Lieutenant Davis had sent to Homicide Detail when he transferred the case), Misco's, and Swenson's, the beat officer who had verified that Lois Palmerston had had dinner with Carol Grogan. Other than Swenson's, none told me anything I didn't know.

When Howard and I got back to our office, Pereira was already there. And she had coffee. In spite of our different assignments, when Howard and I were promoted there had been only one empty office. It had belonged to the community relations officer (before his and his assignment's retirement). He'd complained about what a small, dark hole it was the entire time he had occupied it. Wedging two of us in it didn't make it any more comfortable.

Howard sat in his chair, rolling it back toward the window that was more a symbol than a conveyor of light or air. Small, none too clean, and on the west side of the building, the office got sunlight only from three-thirty till dusk, and then it was so piercing that we closed the blinds. Now the window was like a featureless gray picture on the wall.

I dropped into my own chair, rolling it back against the inside wall. It was a system Howard and I had worked out the second day we shared the office. With the length of Howard's legs, having our backs at the far corners of the floor space was the only way we could both have foot room. When we sat at our desks, facing opposite walls, there was no way we could both back up at once.

Pereira settled atop Howard's desk and pulled out the lower drawer for her feet.

I filled them both in on my interviews. "And you," I said to Pereira, "what did you find out for all your hard work in the bar with Paul Lucas?"

"Not a thing."

"Nothing!"

"It's not that I didn't find out anything. I discovered that there was nothing to find out. Ralph Palmerston was a rich man with no more than peripheral contact with the business world—Chamber of Commerce, social functions, charities—that sort of thing. It took Paul quite a while to place him at all, and for Paul, that's saying something."

I sighed. "Somebody went to a lot of trouble to kill this man, and as far as I can find out, there's no reason at all, unless his wife wanted to inherit. He was even going out of his way to do something nice for the guy who owns Sunny Sides Up, the health food breakfast place. He was planning a Halloween surprise."

"What about the wife?" Howard said. "Palmerston was older. He was going blind. Maybe she didn't want to be burdened with him and realized that this was her last chance to kill him. If his condition was deteriorating, he wouldn't be driving when he got home from their trip."

"There are easier ways."

"But, Jill, this way she has an alibi."

"Not really," I said. "The friend she had dinner with left her alone while she went to pick up her kids from day care. She could have called Palmerston then."

"Wouldn't he have recognized her voice?" Pereira asked. "He was going blind, not deaf."

"Maybe she disguised it. I don't know. Let's let that wait." I took a swallow of coffee. "The really suspicious thing is that the car was in perfect shape when it left the garage. From the time they say Palmerston left and Lois says he got home, he couldn't have stopped. So the car was nowhere but in his own garage between the servicing and his death. Lois Palmerston says there was no one there but she and Ralph."

"Maybe someone came in from the outside," Pereira suggested.

"The garage door locks."

"Locks can be tampered with," Howard put in.

"It's an automatic door opener. She used it when she got home. The garage door had no marks on it. No one forced his way in."

"How about others means of entry?"

"None, except the door from the kitchen."

In unison we picked up our cups and drank.

I said, "It points to Lois Palmerston. She had the opportunity and the motive and could have had the means. It's just that, well, I can't picture her dealing with anything as grubby as a car engine."

Howard laughed. "How fortunate for you to have such genteel suspects. In my cases, brake fluid would be like ambrosia. I think I've had enough of drug dealers and their foul relations. Even my big dealer, Leon Evans, with his college education and grand tour of the Far East —he's still slime." He stood up, suddenly grinning. "By the way, Jill, have you guessed what my costume is yet?"

"Howard, it's only been a little over twelve hours since we made this bet. Give me a chance."

"Having a hard time, huh? Doesn't matter. You'll never guess."

"Don't be so sure. I know you. I know those strange by-roads of your mind."

"Well, you've only got one day to drive down them. Tomorrow's Halloween." He was still grinning as he walked out.

"What's this contest?" Pereira demanded.

"Howard bet me I couldn't figure out what he'll wear to his party."

"What do you get if you do?"

"If I win, I get his parking spot. I spend so much time looking for a place to park now that I might as well have a part-time job."

Pereira whistled.

"Yesterday I had to park nearly in Oakland. I'm not wearing running shoes for fashion."

"Still, Jill, a parking spot. That's like finding gold."

"Well, Howard can get some more gold. All he needs to do is let the word out that he's willing to park his car in one of the local ladies' driveways. They'll be flooding the desk with offers. On the other hand, I'll become a weatherbeaten hag running through the streets of Berkeley and never get offered a spot. This is my only chance."

"Speaking of the party," Pereira said after a minute, "I got your costume."

"Are you sure it will fit me?"

"Jill, with this type of thing, one size fits all."

"I suppose."

"I even got your magic wand."

"Thanks. Now listen, what I have for you is visits to Palmerston's attorney and accountant. See if you can find anything suspicious in his will or his finances."

"Sure. What are you up to?"

I stood up, prepared to make my exit. "I'm going to a health food restaurant."

Sunny Sides Up was located in one of the newly refurbished storefronts two blocks from campus. The building had housed a Greek take-out, a pizza parlor, and a bead shop several years ago before it burned. Then it had sat empty and boarded up for months before being rebuilt to house more gentrified shops.

I had been past the restaurant but never inside. A place that specialized in eggs was too healthy for me, much less one that served only fertilized eggs. I pulled open the door and walked in. The small room was surprisingly quiet. I could still hear the trucks braking in the street and the students calling to their friends. Here, the loudest noise was subdued Bach. The floor was covered with brown indoor-outdoor carpet of distinctly better quality than the rough green mat Mr. Kepple had put on my floor. Pine tables were adorned with cloth napkins and fresh flowers. Along one wall were padded booths covered in red Naugahyde. And above each table was a sepia-toned photograph of the avenue at the turn of the century and an Art Deco light fixture. Brass railings separated the smoking and non-smoking sections. Sunny Sides Up was the early morning equivalent of a fern bar. I could see why Herman Ott had surmised that this restaurant was Adam Thede's baby. Thede had spent thousands to make it charming. But students grabbing breakfast after class, intent on discussing Spinosa or tribal rites in Borneo, didn't care about brass rails or old photos. For them, the funkier the better. And for health food addicts, once a spot mentioned five-bean salad and tofu omelets, all else was fluff.

When crowded, Sunny Sides Up could seat fifty. Now, at eight-thirty in the morning, groupings totaling ten customers dotted the room.

"Party of one?" a young woman asked me.

"No. I need to talk to Adam Thede."

"He's supervising the chef right now."

"I'm with the police."

Unconsciously, she took a step back. "I'll tell him." She hurried back to the swinging door that led to the kitchen. I noticed as she went through it that it led to another swinging door. No wonder there were no kitchen noises in the dining area. Adam Thede, I thought, must be more appreciated by his customers than his staff.

Thede emerged in a minute. He was a tall, broad-shouldered man with dark curly hair. He looked more like a fullback than a restaurateur. Even as he walked toward me, he surveyed the room, momentarily assessing each group of customers.

"Jill Smith, Homicide Detail." I held out my shield, but Thede waved it away.

"What do you want with me? You don't think we've poisoned . . . ?" He had been smiling—a little joke. But he couldn't bring himself to finish it.

"Ralph Palmerston has been murdered. I need to talk to you about him."

"Who? What? Never met a Ralph Palmerston."

"Do you want to talk out here?"

He whirled and looked toward his customers. They were forking in various green and tan comestibles, uninterested in us. Turning back to me, he said, "My office."

I followed him through the double swinging doors and past bags of rice and potatoes, each large enough to last me a lifetime. A chopping board was covered with leeks, endive, various types of mushrooms, and a number of plants, vegetables presumably, that looked as if they had been buried in the backyard for years. Thede indicated a door that said MANAGER. Inside was a four-by-six room, almost entirely filled with a desk and chair. Four stacking trays were piled at the side of the desk by the wall. On that wall was a poster of a face made from vegetables— tomatoes for cheeks, celery for the nose, and lettuce for the rather wrinkled forehead.

"You want to sit?" He pointed to the desk chair.

"I'll stand."

He moved around the desk and stood behind it. I pulled out my pad. We were two feet apart and both had our backs to the walls.

"I'm going to ask you again, Mr. Thede, how is it you know Ralph Palmerston?"

"I don't. I told you—never met the man." He had a fullback's voice. It bellowed in the tiny room.

"Are you sure? Think."

"Unless I shook his hand in passing or someone brought him to one of my parties. . . . When I host, checking the hors d'oeuvres and watching the bar takes all my time. I don't see guests as anything but open mouths till after midnight. I'm giving a Halloween party tomorrow night and I know I won't get to see half the costumes."

"What about business associations? Palmerston was the heir to the Palmieri Winery."

"I don't belong to any associations. I only have this restaurant. I'm not a businessman, I'm a chef, or I was. Now I'm an entrepreneur." He gave me an ironic smile as if realizing how un-entrepreneurlike he looked.

In contrast to the dining area, this tiny office was dark and ill-ventilated. Already I could feel my back getting clammy.

"Ralph Palmerston went to considerable lengths and expense to find out what was important to you. According to my source, he checked out all your suppliers, found out which were on the up-and-up and which ones you should avoid. According to my source, he was planning to use the information to surprise you. Now my—"

Thede's fist hit the desk. "Big deal! Why didn't he tell me? A week ago I could have used that. If this Palmerston fellow had given it to me *then,* it would have been a real gift."

"How so?"

"Don't you read the papers? Didn't you see the number of empty tables out front?"

I nodded, but Thede didn't seem to notice. "Some of my suppliers are tainted. They're spraying grains with commercial herbicides, putting Malathion on their tomatoes. Look!" He thrust a newspaper at me. "Look—'So-Called Health Food Contaminated.' "

I glanced through the article. "But it says you couldn't have known they were using sprays."

"Customers don't care whether I know or not. This

isn't an honesty contest. The fact that I didn't know their milk comes from cattle who've been fed antibiotics doesn't make that milk any less dangerous for them. This place was packed two weeks ago. Now look at it. I've had to lay off three waitresses."

"Surely in time—"

"In time what? It would be one thing if I had known I was serving non-organic food, but I didn't know. Now even if I mount a campaign and say I have all new suppliers whom I've checked out myself, who's going to believe me? They'll say 'He didn't know before, why should we believe him now?' "

"And if you'd gotten Ralph Palmerston's information a week ago, before this story came out?"

"I could have broken the story. I could have denounced my suppliers. I could have been the one who was protecting Berkeley from tainted food, instead of someone who is foisting it on them." He slumped down in the chair.

"What will you do now?"

"Wait. What else?"

"Do you think this will pass?"

He looked down at his desk calendar. "I don't know. I've got a year's lease, so that gives me another six months to sit and count customers."

"And if things don't get better?"

"I'll close."

"You've put a lot of money into Sunny Sides Up."

"I'll lose a lot of money. Probably have to sell my house and go to work for someone else." Now he stared directly at me. "I waited nearly five years to open this restaurant. I've only been here six months. Do you know how awful it is once you've had your own place, created each entrée, made it the best, to have to take orders, to cook commercial eggs with fake cheese and canned mushrooms? Do you know what it's like to do your best and realize it makes no more difference than your least?

Creating a superb breakfast isn't like doing dinner. People don't reserve months in advance even for the best eggs Florentine. The only chance at expression is in your own restaurant." He dropped his gaze. "So you see, money is a small part of it. And any gifts I could have received are a week late."

But, I thought, as with Ellen Kershon, had it worked out, Ralph Palmerston's gift to Adam Thede would have been perfect.

I asked him where he had been yesterday afternoon—home, alone—then handed him my card and told him to call me if he recalled anything about Ralph Palmerston.

I walked out through the dining area, which now held only four people, and down the avenue to Herman Ott's building.

8

"Someone beat you to it," I said.

Herman Ott looked exactly as he had last night, only more rumpled. If there had ever been a question of what he slept in, it was now answered to my satisfaction. He had come stumbling to the door on my second knock, his eyes half closed, his yellow-and-brown shirttail now completely out of his pants. But behind him on his desk I spotted a mug of coffee and two crullers. It made me think better of him.

"I thought you came to bring me my money." His sarcasm was not veiled.

"By the time Thede got the same information you gave Ralph Palmerston, it was already in the newspaper."

"So?"

"So someone was quicker than you were in checking on the growers. Who was that?"

He started to shrug and stopped before his shoulders lifted half an inch. I could see that the question bothered him. It impugned his professional competence.

"Did the people you talked to say someone had been there asking the same questions?"

"No. Listen, there are a dozen places you could get that information. You don't just go up to the grower and say, 'Excuse me, sir, are you adulterating your soybeans?' You go to the pesticide companies; you check their records. You interview the field workers, the union. There could have been ten detectives there and we'd never have run across each other."

I didn't comment. He didn't believe that any more than I did. "When did you give Ralph Palmerston your report?"

"Listen, I don't—"

"Come on, Ott, I don't have to tell you how suspicious this looks. You had plenty of time to leak it to the papers. You wouldn't even have had to walk far to try a little blackmail."

"Blackmail! Goddamnit, are you saying I'm on the take? I've had my chances, plenty of them. But I don't operate that way. That's how come I'm still living." He glared at me, his flaccid cheeks tightening into ridges and hollows. With more control he said, "That's why I'm still living *here.*"

I believed him. Anyone with any money would have moved long ago. Even a man who doesn't care about his surroundings would like a shower that wasn't down the hall. "So, when did you give Ralph Palmerston your report?"

He hesitated, still glaring, then said, "The tenth."

"That was nearly three weeks ago. Wasn't he satisfied with it?"

"Satisfied! Christ, it was twenty pages."

"Then how come he didn't contact you about the other four members of Shareholders Five?"

He leaned back against the desk. "Got me."

"I don't believe that."

"Your privilege."

"This is a murder—"

"Skip it, I know my rights better than you do. The Berkeley Police Department has been on me for twenty years. You better believe I know how far you can push."

"Look—"

"Talk to me when you've got money in your hand."

I turned and left, nearly stumbling over two refugee children playing a game with sticks in the hallway.

Ott was right; he knew his law. I had gotten as much as I was going to from him, at least until the discretionary fund came through. But I had been wrong in thinking that Ralph Palmerston hadn't paid him. He'd have been paid when he handed in his report.

Even with Ott refusing to devulge more, the report itself might give me a lead to the other subjects, or to Palmerston's intentions for them. Palmerston had no business office, so the report would probably be in his house.

I was tempted to drive up there, but I decided against it. I had left Lois Palmerston in shaky condition last night. She had been planning to take sleeping pills. Waking up a widow, a prominent widow, the day after her husband had been killed, to demand to search her house would be a tricky business. Shareholders Five might well have had nothing to do with Palmerston's murder. It could have been just another charitable gesture on his part. (Or it could have been something else.) But if it hadn't led to his death, then the best suspect I had was Lois herself. It wouldn't hurt to find out more about her, and to find it out from the man who had bought her her Mercedes.

I drove west toward the bay, my thoughts bouncing between Lois Palmerston, Adam Thede, Herman Ott, and Herman Ott's two crullers. It was nine-thirty when I pulled up in front of Munsonalysis.

Munsonalysis occupied the second floor of a modern stucco building in the industrial section of Berkeley. Fifteen years ago this area had been a mixture of old factories and wooden houses. The streets were patch-paved; lawns were littered with cars in various states of disembowelment. Its only attraction then was the easy access to the freeway. But with the advent of small businesses—printing, publishing, and all the computer offshoots—the low rents for commercial space drew Berkeley's young entrepreneurs. The same boys and girls who had marched in the sixties' demonstrations, who had primal screamed and been Rolfed in the seventies, had now wriggled toeholds or even footholds into the commercial world of the eighties. And those toes were planted solidly in southwest Berkeley.

The building occupied half the block. It was beige, three stories, with a blue stripe along the top edge, and resembled a beige brick lying on its side. Between it and its brown-and-blue twin that filled the other half of the block was a courtyard with white metal chairs and tables, and several potted trees that gleamed in the post-rain sun. I walked up the outside metal steps. At the top the door said MUNSONALYSIS.

The reception area was surprisingly small, a no-frills room that fit the southwest Berkeley ethic. The only indulgences were on the receptionist's desk—a phone with a panel of buttons attached, computer, electric pencil sharpener, plastic pencil and pencil clip holder, and a calendar with removable plastic numbers. The woman behind the desk—young, Oriental, with hair well down her back—looked up from a book. "Can I help you?" She glanced almost imperceptibly at my brown herringbone jacket and corduroy slacks.

"I need to speak to Jeffrey. I'm Detective Smith, Berkeley Police."

Her facial muscles changed only the slightest amount but that tiny pulling back and tightening was a statement that she had misjudged my status. I almost smiled.

She picked up the phone, chose one of her panel buttons, pushed, and announced me. "Jeffrey will be with you in a minute. If you'd have a seat . . ." She indicated one of the two minimally padded chairs at the other side of the small room.

I nodded but remained standing, glancing out into the empty courtyard.

It was more like ten minutes when a thin man with receding light brown hair opened the door. He was a bit older than I, probably mid-thirties, a bit taller, probably five foot ten. He looked more like he played squash than lifted weights. His dark brown eyes were small but had an almost bulging quality, as if he had squinted so long that he'd pushed them out of place. And his wide mouth looked crowded between the frown lines on either side.

He extended a hand. "Jeffrey Munson."

I introduced myself and shook his hand.

As I followed him along a narrow corridor past offices and small, round-tabled conference rooms, I was aware of his heavy steps. In spite of the fact that he wore running shoes, he almost trudged. Maybe I had been wrong about his playing squash; maybe he did nothing more athletic in those running shoes than walk down this hall.

His office was at the far corner from the courtyard. Two aluminum windows looked out on the streets. The room was beige. His desk was walnut, as was a large table against the far wall. Vintage posters of Chè Guevara, Huey Newton, and the Free Speech Movement adorned the wall.

"Why are you here?" he asked as I sat down.

"Have you seen today's paper?"

"I don't read newspapers, other than the financial news, of course. It's all slanted."

"Then you may not know that Ralph Palmerston is dead."

His eyes seemed to pop back into their rightful place. Surprised, perhaps, but the look that followed was closer to one of calculation. Then both vanished. "I knew *of* him, of course. But I've never met him."

"Never?"

"Never. We don't travel in the same circles."

"But you do know his wife?"

"Lois, yes." His expression was still neutral.

"You knew her quite well, I understand."

His eyes roamed left to his computer screen, as if he wished it were programmed to provide him the least incriminating answer. "She was a friend of my wife's. Was Palmerston killed?"

"Why do you think that?"

"Because," he said with a tight little grin, "the police wouldn't send a detective out to discuss the natural death of someone I've never met."

"Right. Where were you yesterday afternoon?"

His back stiffened. "In and out."

"Can you be more specific?"

"No. Why should I?"

"Because," I said with a sigh, "Ralph Palmerston was murdered."

"I told you I never met the man. I've told you twice, three times now." He smiled that tight smile again, glancing at his posters. "The man was a parasite. He lived off the labor of the men in the fields. He did nothing for society to make up for the hundreds of thousands a year it gave to him."

It had been years since I'd heard this rhetoric in such vintage form. "He contributed a lot to charities."

"Charity," he snorted, "the salve of the bourgeois conscience."

"Is that how his wife described him?"

"Yes."

"In those words?" I asked, trying to hide my surprise.

He smiled fleetingly—a more natural smile. "Lois told us, my wife and me, actually my ex-wife, but she didn't comprehend what a drain on society he was."

"Why not?"

He swallowed; his wide lips pressed together. "Because Lois has become the same kind of parasite. Maybe she always was."

That didn't sound like the observation of a lover. It *did* sound like an ex-lover or a thwarted lover. "Tell me about her."

He looked at the computer screen. "I've already said more than I intended."

"Intended? Did you expect this interview?"

"No. Why should I? It's just a word choice."

I decided to let that pass. "Mr. Munson, this is a murder investigation. You helped Lois Palmerston buy her car. You overhauled it. Your wife is her closest friend. And you have expressed emotional feelings about both the deceased and his wife. You are involved. So it's past the point where you could ponder what you should or shouldn't divulge. In a murder investigation everything you know is important." I let a moment pass before allowing a small, accommodating smile on my face. Jeffrey Munson might have had the same feelings about the police as Herman Ott, but I was betting that he would be less on guard in dealing with a woman cop, particularly a smiling one. "Start from the beginning. How did you come to know Lois Palmerston?"

"She was in college with my wife. She was Lois Burk then. My wife was her big sister. It's a thing they have at the college. The senior girls sort of watch out for the freshmen. Lois was Nina's freshman."

"And after college, did they keep in touch?" I prompted.

"We were in New York City then. Lois stayed with us. She was looking for acting jobs. They're damned hard to come by no matter how much talent you have."

That sounded more loverlike. "Did Lois have talent?"

"I don't know. I never saw her act. She did some work in a few pieces of fluff off-Broadway, nothing of any social consequence, nothing worth seeing."

"But she did get jobs? She must have had something going for her."

"But not enough to support herself. She lived with us on and off for four years. In some of the apartments we had it was damned crowded."

"And then what happened?"

"We came out here."

"Lois didn't come with you?"

"No. Actually she almost did. It was her idea. She was such a user. She got caught up in the idea of California. She thought she'd try the movies. She thought there would be more opportunities for her here. She got Nina all caught up in it. Nina really was a big sister to her. Nina had a good job. She was editing a poetry magazine in the Village. You can imagine how often a job like that comes along. It didn't pay much but it paid. But Lois convinced her that California was where the *muse* was. Lois convinced her that I could work in computers anywhere. So Nina came out here to check things out. And by the time she'd had a look at L.A. and then come to Berkeley and found a place, Lois had a part in a play and wasn't about to move."

"But you did?"

"Everything was already in the works."

I leaned back, crossed my legs, and decided to postpone guessing whether he was Lois's lover, former lover, would-be lover, or would-have-been lover. "When Lois did come out here, where did she stay?"

"Where else? With us. But at least this time it was only for two months."

"Why was that?"

"She moved to the city."

"Where in San Francisco?"

He looked at the computer screen. His finger caressed the ERASE key. "Pacific, near Octavia. She got a job in the city."

Hammonds architectural firm would have to have paid their receptionists—or "customer relations"—people very well indeed, I thought. Pacific and Octavia were in Pacific Heights, the old-moneyed section of the city. It was a definite step up from having to stay with friends.

"She said you got her her car."

His finger moved back to the ERASE key.

"When was that?" I prodded.

"Right after she moved to the city."

In Berkeley one could get along without a car, but life was easier with one. In San Francisco, parking was such a hassle and public transportation so convenient, that driving was a luxury, if not an added problem. The only thing you needed a car for in the city was to leave it. Had Jeffrey Munson found Lois the car so she could drive to Berkeley? To see him? "Why did you get Lois the Mercedes?"

He tapped the ERASE key. "It was used. I got a good deal for her. It needed a lot of work. It had been owned by some rich parasite in the hills. He had two Ferraris in the garage. He left the Mercedes standing out summer and winter. The finish was down to rust. And the engine! You couldn't see out the back window when you started it, the emissions were so black. It needed a lot of work. That's why the guy was selling it. Of course, he had no idea how to fix it. Why would he, he didn't even know how to keep it up."

"How long did it take you to get it in shape?"

"Let's see, I got it in the middle of the summer. Lois needed it in September. So even with Nina helping, it probably took me a month. I had to hit the junkyards for used parts. And then the finish takes a long time with the drying and all. I had to take three days off work but I got it done. Her mechanic said it was a better job than they do in most shops," he said proudly. "I worked as a mechanic's assistant for a couple of months when I first got here, so I know he was right." In contrast to his wooden demeanor when denouncing parasites, now those deep frown lines lifted, pulling his wide mouth up into a smile of remembrance.

I leaned forward over the desk. "Mr. Munson, let me ask you this. You've told me Lois made use of both you and your ex-wife when you were in New York and in engineering your move out here. Then she came and stayed with you for two months. You let her. And then, Mr. Munson, you spent all that time redoing an expensive car for her. Why?"

Deliberately, he moved his hand away from the computer. "My wife, ex-wife, Nina, was her big sister. No one could complain about Lois in front of Nina. For Nina, whatever Lois took she must have needed, she must have had a reason for everything she demanded. It was just easier not to argue."

"Are you sure that's all?"

"What do you mean?"

"Well, Mr. Munson, another interpretation of these events would be that you found yourself attracted to Lois. She's a beautiful woman. You—"

"Hey, just a minute—"

I put up a hand. "Let me finish. Lois stayed with you in New York. And when one of the three of you left, it wasn't Lois, it was your wife. Maybe she moved to California and forced you to choose between her and Lois."

"Well, I came out here, didn't I?"

Passing over his comment, I went on. "And then after you settled here, Lois comes and stays with you again. And then you and your wife get a divorce. You can see where it might look—"

"But it wasn't! I told you what a parasite Lois was. Do you think I could get it on with a woman like that? She was Nina's friend. Nina insisted Lois stay with us out here. Nina wanted me to get the car. Nina even helped do the work on it. If it hadn't been for Nina, Lois could have stayed at the YWCA."

I made a show of writing notes. But it hadn't been his explanations so much as his enthusiasm talking about helping Lois when she came out here that made the statement. "Wasn't your wife working then?"

"She worked at home. She was a seamstress. She designed and made women's clothes."

There was a world of difference between a seamstress and a designer. "I thought she was a poet."

"Yes. I assumed you meant work—money-making."

I closed the note pad. "Mr. Munson, for whatever reason, you've done a lot for Lois Palmerston over the years. Didn't it seem odd to you that she never had you to her house to meet her husband?"

"What does that have to do with his death?" His finger pressed the ERASE key. There was a soft thump; the machine was turned off.

"Right now everything has to do with his death. And that lack of reciprocity stands out."

"Well, it wasn't any *lack of reciprocity*. Lois asked us to dinner but I wasn't going to go and drink champagne with a parasite like Ralph Palmerston. How do I know where his money comes from. Maybe I would have been eating caviar paid for with money made in non-union vineyards. I run my business within strict guidelines. We do subsidiary projects for larger firms. But I don't take contracts from defense contractors or exploiters. I can tell you that I've turned down thousands of dollars of business. I could have put Munsonalysis in the black if I'd taken them. And if I don't accept work from parasites, I'm certainly not going to drink with them."

All Munson's views fitted the well-fed radical line, but there was something about him that didn't click. I stood up. "One more thing, Mr. Munson, when was the last time you saw Lois Palmerston?"

He started to speak, then caught himself. "I was going to say not since she got married, but that isn't right. I ran into her in the spring, downtown, and we had a drink. I thought then that she had really become Mrs. Palmerston. I wouldn't see her again."

9

White-collar firms had a solid hold on southwest Berkeley where Munsonalysis was, but cafés had not yet joined them. Now at ten-fifteen when I wanted to ponder what Jeffrey Munson had and had not told me, all I could think of was Herman Ott's crullers. Fortunately, San Pablo Avenue, which runs through every town north of Oakland like a string holding synthetic pearls, is the fast-food mecca of the East Bay. Finding two jelly doughnuts and coffee took me less than three minutes. I sat in my car, coffee cup on the opened glove compartment door. Biting carefully into the doughnut so the ersatz jelly wouldn't squirt onto my face, or, God forbid, my only remaining clean blouse, I considered Jeffrey Munson. Despite what he had said, he had all the markings of a rejected lover or at least a rejected would-be lover. After all, it wasn't unknown for a man to be attracted by something other than a woman's political views. Had Lois led Jeffrey on till she had gotten what she needed from him? Had he indeed been her lover? Was he still? Why not an affair that had lasted through Lois's marriage till the marriage itself became a hindrance? Why not Jeffrey, entering the house with Lois's key before Ralph Palmerston got home from the Cadillac agency? Jeffrey could have hidden inside till Ralph pulled into the garage, got out of the car, and came in through the kitchen. Once Ralph

went to another part of the house, most likely the bedroom to change, or the bathroom, it would have been
easy for Jeffrey to slip into the garage and cut the brake
lines. He had had plenty of experience with cars. Then he
could have hidden in the back of Lois's car. When she
left to dine with her friend, she could have dropped him
off wherever they chose.

In a year, would Lois and Jeffrey marry, after *renewing
their friendship?* Would Lois invest in Munsonalysis and
finally put it in the black?

Lois Palmerston and Jeffrey Munson were not a pair I
would have picked from a crowd. Lois looked like a rose;
Jeffrey the thorn. But who was I to say what would appeal to someone else? After my divorce, I had realized I
didn't even know what was good for me. But whatever
the attraction, the key to Jeffrey and Lois's relationship
was Nina Munson.

Nina Munson lived in a flat with the address of 1733C
Gilroy Street. In a North Berkeley neighborhood of
small, single-family stucco houses set in yards that rarely
had more than five feet between the house and property
line, creating three extra dwellings was no mean accom-
plishment. In all likelihood, building codes had been broken right and left as they were built, and new violations
of the housing codes had been created with occupancy. I
was just glad that Mr. Kepple didn't know what possibili-
ties had eluded him.

The house numbered 1733 was a typical pink stucco
split-level, with the living room to the left of the dining
room-cum-entryway in the middle and the bedrooms
over the garage at the right. A walkway to the right of
that led to 1733 A, B, and C.

Apartment A turned out to be the rear of the two
bedrooms over the garage. An outside staircase had been
added that ended in a deck at what once must have been
the bedroom window. B looked like two large utility

sheds joined together and set directly behind the living room. Since the living room was six feet above ground level, the rear windows looked out on the shed roof. It ran twenty or so feet back to the east property line and looked more suitable for rakes and manure than for people. C was an eight-by-twenty-five stucco rectangle that filled the space five feet south of B to the south property line. It had the potential to be as unappealing as B, but window boxes, a Japanese maple in a large redwood container, and a slate patio gave it an almost cozy look.

The door was oak, stripped and varnished. A stained glass window of a prancing bird filled much of the upper half. I knocked.

"It's open."

I stepped in. Two-thirds of the unit formed one oblong room. The remaining third was divided between kitchen and bath. The only window in the main room was a wind-out aluminum one set in the front wall. It was a dwelling in which a monk would have felt no guilt.

But Nina Munson had decorated with the artist's touch. Opposite the window was an almost-antique "fainting couch," which held a pile of elaborate patchwork jackets with the store tags already on their sleeves. Above it she had eight-by-ten photos of samples of her work—more patchwork jackets, coats, cloaks, and vests. All but one were brightly colored garments like the ones on the couch. The remaining one was a white-on-white appliqué gown. On the floor was an old but still colorful Oriental rug.

There was no closet (one housing code violation). An antique oak coatrack stood in the corner by the bathroom sporting what looked like all of Nina's clothes—paisley-patched corduroy pants, embroidered denim skirt, white painting overalls and jacket, peasant blouse, Peruvian sweater, Irish knit sweater dyed kelly green, and multicolored garments underneath, which I couldn't quite make out. Had my clothes been hooked on a rack like that for the world to see, they would have looked merely like a pile of laundry. But Nina's seemed as if they had been hung by Mary Cassatt.

By the window was a sewing machine and a large table covered with pieces of fabric. Next to the window, on the wall, were pinned sketches of a Japanese jacket. Glancing down at the table, I could see the beginnings of the jacket pinned together.

"I'm Detective Smith, Berkeley Police, Homicide Detail." I extended my shield.

"Homicide?" She ignored the shield.

"It's about Ralph Palmerston's death."

"Ralph Palmerston died?"

Didn't anyone read the paper? "He was killed in an auto crash yesterday. We have some questions about it."

"But Homicide? That means murder." She stared at me as if trying to piece together what I had said. Nina Munson was a small, dark woman with short, blunt-cut, almost black hair, and small features that seemed to congregate in the center of her face. Her shoulders were rounded, probably from stooping forward over her sewing machine. She looked like a troll who had wandered into the brightly decorated flat. Everything in the flat was beautiful except her.

"Lois's husband was murdered?" she asked.

"I gather Lois hasn't called you."

"No."

"She said you were her closest friend."

Nina Munson looked up and smiled. "She did? Odd."

"Why odd?"

"We were friends in college but I haven't seen her much since she married. But in college she was my little sister," she added quickly. I recalled Jeffrey Munson saying that Nina always made excuses for Lois. "The school set up the big sister thing between senior girls and freshmen. For Lois it was a good arrangement. There were a lot of girls from wealthy families at Binghamton. That area of Connecticut has a lot of money. But Lois and I were both scholarship kids. Neither of us had the money to go on ski weekends or to Florida for spring vacation. When Lois's friends were gone I was there for her. I knew how to cut corners, how to make money last."

"But you haven't seen her since her marriage?" I asked. "Was that because of Jeffrey? Were Lois and Jeffrey lovers?"

I wouldn't have been surprised if she had been outraged by my question. What she did was laugh. "Jeffrey? Jeffrey, the leftover radical, involved with a rich lady, a member of the Establishment? Jeffrey would be humiliated."

"But you and Jeffrey did get a divorce after Lois lived with you."

"It wasn't because of Lois. Jeffrey and I were too different. We wanted different things. College masks reality, and what appeals to you there often seems ridiculous in the adult world. Let me tell you about Jeffrey. Jeffrey was one of those kids who never fit in. He had pimples; he was soft. You know the type."

I nodded.

"But in college, he discovered radical politics. It wasn't that he was political per se, or particularly concerned about the oppressed; what he wanted was friends. And campus radical groups would accept anyone who was willing to carry a sign. So, for Jeffrey, radicalism had all the unfocused emotional qualities of Mom and home."

Clearly this was a topic she had given a lot of thought. That was hardly surprising; I had given my ex-husband more thought than I would have admitted during our separation and divorce. I'd pondered his failings; I'd bored my friends with his faults; I'd refused his phone calls, and then had screaming fights in the middle of the night. I'd behaved like a jerk. Compared to me, Nina Munson's sudden explosion of words about her ex was the height of good sportsmanship.

"Jeffrey's problem was that radicalism was so much an ingrained emotional need, that he never could bring himself to question whether he really believed the doctrine."

"What do you mean?"

"He sends money to the rebels in Central America. He votes for every minority candidate on the ballot. But the only minority employee he has is his receptionist. He's all for integrated housing, but he lives so high in the hills that the only blacks who ever see his house are the ones being bussed to public works projects in Tilden Park. The thing about Jeffrey is that he loves the poor, but only from a distance."

I glanced around the small, cavelike apartment.

Nina laughed. "You're thinking that if Jeffrey wanted to see how the poor live, he could come here?"

That was exactly what I was thinking.

"For a while, pretending to be poor appealed to Jeffrey. He liked the idea of being married to an artist, of living on nothing. He was impressed by how easily I could make do. He even liked"—she paused—"the fact that I wasn't pretty. It showed how much he supported the underdog." She stared as if daring me to contradict her. "He liked being married to the girl who had faced down the college dean. We were demonstrating for autonomy in inviting speakers to campus. I read him the demands. I got a little carried away. And I got expelled. Jeffrey was impressed, but he wasn't willing to jeopardize his college degree to join me." She shrugged. "Maybe it's just as well. Jeffrey needed that degree to get into computers. And if it weren't for the money from Munsonalysis, little as it is, neither of us could live."

"Were Jeffrey and Lois lovers?" I asked again.

She looked down at the amber cloth on her lap. It was nearly a minute before I realized that she wasn't going to answer.

"Jeffrey did a lot for Lois," I said. "He overhauled an entire car for her."

Nina sighed. "Oh, that. I see what you're thinking. It does sound like Jeffrey put himself out. But you should understand that if it were helping her buy a fridge or look for a job, Jeffrey wouldn't have considered it. Jeffrey loves cars. When we were first married, and I was being the dutiful wife, I helped him overhaul two Buicks and a vintage Ford, inside and out. He spent every night of the week on those cars. Even now the Porsche he drives has an entirely rebuilt engine. Jeffrey left only the exterior as is so he wouldn't look too successful."

It was becoming clear to me that whatever there might have been between Lois and Jeffrey, no one was going to admit it. I asked, "What was Ralph Palmerston like?"

"I don't know."

"Didn't you meet him?"

"No."

"Not even at the wedding?"

"No."

I waited.

"He had a yacht then. Maybe he still does. It was a small wedding for his special friends."

"But Lois said you were her closest friend."

She shrugged. "I wouldn't exactly fit in with moneyed society. And Jeffrey would have felt obliged to make an ass of himself. Lois made a wise choice."

"Well, how did Lois and Ralph Palmerston get along?"

"I don't know. I haven't seen her much since her marriage. I called her a few times and we had a drink. But I always had to call her. You know how that is."

I started to respond, but she interrupted me. "You're going to say that seems odd for someone who stayed with me. It probably does to you. But I'm an odd person. Odd things don't bother me. I live here because I like it. If I chose to work at a regular job, I could make more money than I do selling designer jackets, and certainly more than I do writing poetry. I had to sell my mother's antique necklace five years ago. I didn't think I could bear to part with it. But once it was gone, I felt free. The only really odd thing about meeting with Lois was that I called her. I don't know why I did that. It was after the divorce. Maybe I was in a period of adjustment. Maybe I had to see what still existed or what never existed."

Maybe, I thought, you wanted to find out what had gone on between Lois and Jeffrey. I said, "Ralph Palmerston was murdered. Do you have any idea why?"

"No."

"Where were you yesterday afternoon?"

I expected her to be taken aback by my implied suspicion, but she answered in the same way she had all the other questions. "Right here."

"Did you see or talk to anyone?"

"No."

"No one? Not even the mailman?"

"No. Sometimes days go by when I don't utter a word. It's a kind of control of my environment that most people can't have. I like it that way."

I noted that Nina Munson had no alibi. I said to her, "Lois told me you were her closest friend. Even considering what you've just said about her, you must know her as well as anyone. Do you think she is capable of murder?"

Again, she looked neither shocked nor offended. "It's hard to imagine anyone we know killing her husband. But those things happen. About Lois, I couldn't give you an opinion."

Leaving her my card, I told her to call me if she thought of anything that would help. She said she would.

I stood by the door, looking back at the pile of jackets on the fainting couch with their price tags hanging in a line from their sleeves. To Nina, I said, "Shareholders Five? What does that mean to you?"

"Nothing. Should it?"

"Ralph Palmerston was planning to do something nice for five people. I wondered if you were one of them."

She tilted her head slightly to one side and smiled. "Well, I haven't noticed anything. But maybe he was concentrating on people who need things."

Closing the door behind me, I walked across the slate patio and along the path beside 1733 to my car. Nina and Jeffrey Munson had given me a different picture of Lois Palmerston than I had had last night, closer to a predator than a victim. And no matter whom I talked to, everything led back to the Palmerston house.

Now it was after ten-thirty, time for even a grieving widow to be up. Time for me to see Ralph Palmerston's copy of Herman Ott's report.

10

It took me fifteen minutes to maneuver up the now-familiar corkscrew route to the top of the hills. I pulled up beside Lois's driveway.

When I got out of my car, I stood for a moment, looking at that view I had known last night would be spectacular. It was the reason that a house that would sell for well under one hundred thousand dollars in Cleveland went for between three and four hundred thousand on this street. In the after-storm brightness, the cloudless sky shone with the translucence of a Tiffany lamp. Sunlight bounced off the still-wet acacias and London plane trees down the hillside. Below the hills, in the flats, the white stucco houses sparkled. San Francisco Bay glistened. The Bay Bridge arched like a silver filigree necklace, dropping down onto the kelly green of Treasure Island, the mound of land that engineers had created to house the 1939 Golden Gate International Exposition. Sailboats with Clorox-white mainsails meandered between the bright green of Angel Island, where the deer still roamed free, and Alcatraz, where you could now take tours to see how it was to be less fortunate than the deer. And there was the skyline of San Francisco, and the Golden Gate Bridge.

Few days were as clear as this, with air as clean, sun as bright. And fewer still was I up this high in the hills to survey the whole Bay Area. I wondered if Lois Palmerston, who had this view for the asking, still found it wonder-inspiring.

I walked beside the stucco courtyard wall that ran from the garage to the living room. I pressed the bell next to the gate.

The living room windows looked just as they had last night—lower shutters drawn. Done for privacy, I assumed, since every fabric in the living room was white—nothing to fade there.

Behind me the street was silent. Leaves hung motionless in the still morning. I glanced across at the Kershon house, wondering if Billy had escaped pneumonia and was back in school boasting to his friends that he was the last person to see his neighbor alive.

"Oh, it's you." Lois Palmerston stood in her doorway. She was wearing the same raw silk pants and silk sweater she had had on last night. Her reddish-blond hair was still drawn back in combs, but clumps of hair had escaped and hung at odd angles. She looked like the "before" picture of the woman I had seen last night. Her clothes didn't look slept in; they appeared limp, used. The makeup that had so subtly accentuated her even features and her slightly arched nose last night had faded in the night hours, allowing the dark circles under her eyes to take preeminence. She reached a hand inside the doorway to push the gate release.

The gate swung open and I walked toward her. "Have you slept at all?" I asked.

"No. I didn't expect to."

"Have you eaten?"

A sardonic smile flashed on her face. "I smoked. It's better than food."

She didn't have to tell me; the stench of smoke from the house was almost overwhelming. It had been barely noticeable last night; she must have chain-smoked in the intervening hours. Even now as she stood in the doorway, her hand shook as she rested it on the door frame.

"I need to talk to you," I said.

"I can't talk now. I'm in no shape to talk. I . . ."

"You what?"

"I have to force myself to work out complete sentences."

My first reaction was to tell her she needed to sleep. But I had to get inside the house. I said, "It's important."

Her eyes seemed so pale now that I wondered if she had been wearing tinted contact lenses last night. "I can't."

"Mrs. Palmerston, your husband has been murdered. Someone deliberately cut the brake lines on his car."

I looked for a response, a revealing one. But she merely nodded as if I'd told her the laundry would be late.

"Time is vital. I'm sure you want your husband's murderer caught."

She nodded again, as if it were all right to have the sheets and towels returned even later.

"Can I come in?"

She didn't move. "What do you want to know?"

"I need to see your husband's rooms, his things." I wanted to find Ott's report.

"Oh, you can't do that. Not his rooms. I can't, not yet."

"You don't need to come with me. I can go through the house alone. If I have to ask you—"

"No. Not now. Too soon." She patted her slacks pocket for cigarettes. Finding none, her hand went back to the door frame. Her arm barred my way.

It was a touchy situation. I couldn't force my way in, not legally. Bullying a distraught widow, a rich socialite with influential friends, could cause more problems than it was worth. If she didn't let me in, I could try for a warrant, or I could wait.

"Mrs. Palmerston," I said, "I realize that it's difficult

for you to think about mundane things, but I need to know what your husband was doing. Tell me about him and Adam Thede?"

When she didn't react, I went on. "About Shareholders Five?" Still no reaction. She hadn't even blinked. Taking a breath, I tried a less promising tack, but one which she could handle. "Tell me about your finances—before your marriage."

She stared at me with those colorless eyes. "Maybe later."

I shifted my weight. "A lot of questions are difficult when you're upset, but you can tell me about yourself. Those things you *know.*" Without waiting for a response, I asked, "What jobs did you have before you came to California?"

"In New York?"

"Right."

She looked at me blankly.

"What was your longest running play?"

"Look, I told you I can't think straight."

"Did you support yourself acting?"

"Sometimes."

"And the rest of the time?"

"I did temporary jobs."

"Where?"

"A number of places. I was there for eight years."

"Specifically?"

"Look, this is just the type of thing I can't think of. If you want to know the where and when of things, you'll have to talk to me later."

"You can't remember anywhere you worked in eight years?" I asked, astounded.

"Okay. Bloomingdale's."

"When?"

"Christmas."

"Which Christmas?"

"I don't know. Leave me alone. Can't you see I'm falling apart?"

I took a breath. "Just one more question. When you came here, you stayed with Nina and Jeffrey Munson for a while, then you got an apartment in Pacific Heights. You bought a Mercedes, used, but still a Mercedes. How did you have the money for that?

"Savings."

"From jobs?"

"Yes."

"Which—"

"I can't. . . . No more." She shut the door.

I stood for a moment. It isn't often that a police detective gets the door slammed in her face. I wondered if Lois Palmerston was as frazzled as she appeared. Was she so exhausted that she'd shut the door on a police officer without thinking? Or was she well aware of her protected position, and one sharp lady?

11

For a nice man who spent his time raising money for charities, Ralph Palmerston certainly had suspicious relatives, acquaintances, and non-acquaintances. This morning I had talked to five people, all of whom had something fishy about them. I wasn't surprised they were holding back. I couldn't recall a murder investigation where any suspect or witness had been completely open with me. I doubted that in their place I would have been very trusting. I only wished I knew what it was they were hiding and whether those carefully protected nuggets of their pasts had anything to do with Palmerston's murder.

I coasted to a stop at the top of University Avenue, then made a right onto it. At Martin Luther King Junior Way, I watched four cars run the red light before I turned left. The intersection badly needed a left turn signal. There was no way to make a left there except against the light, and even with two cars breaking the law on each red, a driver could wait ten minutes to clear the intersection onto University. Somehow the system seemed very Berkeley—a utilitarian scofflawing accepted by all.

I made a left onto McKinley. The station was to my left. To my right were cars, parked up to the edges of driveways, parked in those driveways. I slowed to first gear, not really expecting to find a parking spot this close to the station but unable to make myself give up hope and begin my search three blocks away.

Adam Thede was a chef turned entrepreneur with more impulsiveness than sense. According to him he hadn't known Ralph Palmerston, and Palmerston's gift of information had come too late to save him. Herman Ott hadn't contradicted that. Nor had he confirmed it. I didn't believe Palmerston had given Ott only one of the names of Shareholders Five. Ott knew I didn't. And there that stood.

As for Jeffrey Munson (I helped Lois only because my wife wanted me to), Nina Munson (I mothered her for twelve years but it doesn't matter that she hasn't bothered with me since she married money), and Lois herself, I didn't know where to fit them in. Jeffrey knew more than enough about cars to have dealt with Ralph's. Lois had balanced precariously on the edge of insolvency for years until she lucked into meeting Ralph.

I crossed the intersection. Was that a spot ahead? I stepped on the gas before the car coming from the other end of the street could get to it.

"Damn!" A white curb! Loading zone. How many times had I made this mistake? I kept forgetting about the day-care center and its seductive loading zone. I stepped hard on the accelerator and passed the filled curbs on the rest of the block.

One block down and two over I wedged the Volkswagen between two pickup trucks. My rear bumper was an inch in front of one, five or six inches behind the other. It had taken me five tries to get in. I climbed out of the car, slammed the door, and began a loping run to the station.

When I passed the official car lot, I spotted Howard loading Leon Evans, his educated drug dealer, into a squad car.

"Good-looking buns, sugar," Evans called.

I turned, glaring.

Howard shoved him in the car and slammed the door. Then he ambled toward me, grinning.

I stopped, panting.

"Consider that high praise," Howard said. "Evans doesn't have the best manners but he is a connoisseur of the female form. He doesn't acknowledge the mediocre."

Still panting, I aimed my glare at him. It only made him laugh harder, and I could feel a smile creeping onto my face. I pursed my lips to hold it back. I wasn't about to give Howard the satisfaction of making me laugh. "You want something?"

"Maybe this isn't the best time. Maybe when you've billy-clubbed a couple of prisoners, you'll be in better spirits."

I wiped the sweat from my forehead. "What is it?"

He looked away. The grin was still in place. "A favor," he said in a small voice.

"What kind of favor?"

"Personal."

"You mean on my lunch break?"

"Yeah." His voice was lower, his grin broader. He knew whatever it was, I would do it for him. "It's the liquor store. I've got to pay for the booze for the party tomorrow. No payment, no delivery. Working here didn't impress them any. Now"—he put a hand on my shoulder —"you're thinking why can't this slob deal with this on his own lunch break? He's probably eaten a much more decent breakfast than I have, right? So I'll tell you. I have to spend the next couple of hours with our friend in the car. I'll take him to his place, trot on in with him, and spend long enough in there to give his associates something to think about."

That sounded like a Howard job. With his height, his curly red hair, his "cop" look, whenever anything needed to be noticed, Howard was the one chosen. "Okay."

He fished in his pocket and extricated his wallet.

"Here's my VISA. This note says I give you permission to sign for it."

I glanced at the note. " 'To Whom It May Concern,' eh? You sure you won't get your next bill from the Mexico City Hilton?"

"You do that and I'll give Leon Evans your address there." Evans, as if hearing his name, was banging on the squad car window. "It's going to be a long couple hours," Howard said, turning toward the car.

Pocketing his VISA, I headed into the station. I had been planning to dictate my interviews, hoping that would put them in some order for me. Now I just checked my IN box—it held one note from Pereira: *Palmerston's accountant confirms all assets in commercial stocks. No blocks big enough for influence. C.P.*

My eyes wandered to Howard's box. Last night when I looked over his messages, I had had a pang of guilt. Today, after my latest parking safari and Evans's assessment of my derriere, I had no such qualms. But again, there was no hint of Howard's costume there.

Leaving a note that I would be back by one, I stalked out in disgust. Maybe he already had his costume. Maybe it was hanging in his closet. Maybe I should have the liquor delivered to his house now and accompany it with a search of his room. After all, there were no ground rules on this bet. But I couldn't believe it was there. I knew most of Howard's roommates. Considering their all-around flakiness, I doubted he would trust them with any clue of it, much less the costume itself. Howard knew me too well to think I wouldn't give them a try.

I crossed Martin Luther King Junior Way. Then where was that costume? Howard was six foot six. His costume was no small item. It couldn't be stuffed in his glove compartment. I doubted it would even fit in his trunk, with all the junk he kept in there. At a friend's house? No, the logical place would still be in the costume store, with strict instructions that it wasn't to be revealed to anyone but Howard.

There was only one costume store in Berkeley—California Costumery. Costumers were used to secrecy. They wouldn't reveal Howard's secret. But I had a surprise for them.

I walked the remaining blocks to my car, finished the five tries getting it out of the space, and drove to the liquor store smiling. Ten minutes later I had used Howard's VISA to pay for his liquor and arrived at California Costumery.

No place is as mobbed as a costume store the day before Halloween. California Costumery occupied a small showroom, with a large dressing room behind it and a storage area to the right. The showroom was a ten-foot wooden square sporting an old display case filled with noses, beaks, and snouts, bunny tails and bow ties, pointed ears, floppy ears, and mustaches of all colors. On the wall were rubbery masks of Father Time, Ebenezer Scrooge, of gorillas, goblins, purple-faced spooks, and witches in pasty white. Above them perched rebel hats, cowboy hats, fedoras, and rainbow-head wigs. Standing in the corner were canes, bludgeons (presumably of crepe paper and tin foil), broomsticks, and a selection of tails that would have inspired Beelzebub.

And in the room were at least twenty people with looks of such desperation that Halloween costumes hardly seemed necessary.

I took a number and settled under the sign that prohibited checks during the Halloween rush.

A man of about twenty at the desk was explaining that nothing but a bald head with an orange fringe of hair would do. He already had a Day-Glo black T-shirt.

I figured I'd be here awhile. I might as well do that ordering of my thoughts that I had passed over at the station. Back to the basics on the Palmerston case—Who gained? Lois inherited. She had no money of her own (as far as I knew—I would have to check further on that). But Nina and Jeffrey Munson both said, loosely translated, that she had become acclimated to wealth. Maybe she could do without Ralph, but not without his money.

The bald-and-orange-wigged man moved on and was replaced by three women with urges to be Stooges. They, the harried clerk told them, were in luck. She called to a woman and pointed the three to the dressing room.

Jeffrey, the anxious lover? He might want to kill Ralph Palmerston, but why choose now?

At the counter, a tall man asked to be done as a king. "Where I'm going," he said, "there'll be plenty of queens."

What about Nina murdering Ralph? That didn't make sense. You don't kill a man because his wife hasn't called you.

"Miss?"

I looked up.

"Can I help you?"

I stood up. "I'm sorry. I thought there were so many people ahead of me."

The clerk, a young black woman wearing a halo and glitter-covered cape, laughed. "You got a dragon there. Like Chinese New Year. All seven of them. I tell you, it's going to be a long night for the dudes in the middle."

"Probably for everyone else, too. I hope they're not going where I am."

"What can I get you?" She glanced over my body and I had the feeling she was playing a private guessing game as to whether I would be half a horse or Marie Antoinette.

"I'm here to pick up a costume. The name's Seth Howard."

Her eyes narrowed. "You Seth Howard?"

"No."

"Sorry. We can't give costumes to anyone but the customer. See?" She pointed to a sign under the one forbidding checks. "We've got our customers' trust to uphold."

"I understand. But he got caught up and asked me to pick it up for him."

"Sorry. No exceptions." She pointed to the sign again.

I pulled out Howard's VISA card and his note authorizing me to use it, and handed them to her. "He'll appreciate your precautions. And he wouldn't trust anyone but me with the costume."

She studied the note, then handed it and the card back to me. "Okay. Seth Howard. Hang on." She floated past me, sparkling cape flying out behind her.

I smiled. The really fine thing about getting Howard's costume this way was that he himself had made it possible. Should I leave it at his house with a note—just my name? But I knew I couldn't wait. I'd take it back to our office now and plop it in his lap. Then I'd go out and move my car into his garage.

Still smiling, I looked around. In the near corner of the dressing room a Quasimodo hump expanded on the back of a five-foot-six man. From the doorway the dragon stuck its head out, then pulled it back abruptly and collapsed to the floor. Six bare legs were visible. A voice reiterated, "It's got to be coordinated, dummy. Right foot first."

It was a few minutes before the clerk returned, looking more harried than before. "No," she said.

"Not ready?"

"Not here. You were so certain, so I checked all our files. You must have the wrong place. There's no costume for a Seth Howard. No one ordered one. No one picked one up. No one canceled one. This Seth Howard ought to get his head straight before he sends people chasing around."

"Are you sure?"

"I just told you—"

"I know, I know. Maybe it's my fault. Where else do they rent costumes?"

"They may have some left in San Francisco."

"None in the East Bay?"

"Halloween comes only once a year. How many people you think it can support?"

I shrugged. "Thanks."

"Sure."

"Damn," I muttered as I walked outside. "Damn, damn." If his costume wasn't here, where could it be? He had to be having it made privately. And if that was the case, there was no way I could find it. I couldn't call every seamstress in the Bay Area. I'd better just save my money for a new pair of running shoes.

When I got back to the station, I looked for Pereira, but she was out. I checked my IN box, hoping for another note from her. But what I found was a message from the Detective Division secretary: *Inspector Doyle wants to see you at 2:00.*

12

Detective Inspector Frederick Doyle had been in charge of Homicide Detail before I had joined the force, long before the proposition of being a cop had even occurred to me. Compared to Oakland and San Francisco, we didn't have many murders in Berkeley, even with this latest spurt of killings (most of them were drug-related, it was turning out). But Doyle kept his eye on every investigation. And our record of File Closed's was impressive. Unsolved cases ate at him. He was reputed to be able to list them all, all the way back to the sixties. And he was said to be able to name the officers who had failed to solve them.

I'd met the inspector, of course. He'd interviewed me for the Homicide position. But I had yet to present a case to him. Now, at one-thirty, I wished that I had stayed in and dictated reports on my morning interviews instead of wasting my time at California Costumery. Inspector Doyle wouldn't have expected that—it would be unrealistic—but it would have looked good. Barring that, at least I could decide what to emphasize—which suspect, which lead—when I talked to him.

But before I could reach for my pad, there was a knock on the door. Almost simultaneously it opened and Clayton Jackson's head jutted around the edge. "You in, Detective?"

"Yeah, but I'm boning up to see Doyle in half an hour."

Jackson ambled in and plopped into Howard's chair. Clayton Jackson was one of the two regular Homicide detectives. He had been in Homicide when I started on the force four years ago. I had the impression he had been new to it then, but I wasn't sure. With the other Homicide man, Al Eggenberger, "Eggs" of course, Jackson made an unusual pairing. Eggs was in his mid-thirties, blond, and looked more like an MBA than a cop. In contrast, Clayton Jackson was the blackest man I'd ever seen. He was a bit short of six feet, barrel-chested, and, to take him at his word, could stare down any con in Alameda County.

"How's it going?" he asked.

"I don't know. I've got a philanthropist murdered before he could go blind, a wife who inherits, and a note in the glove compartment saying Shareholders Five, a group that, according to Herman Ott—"

Jackson groaned.

"—included Adam Thede, who owns that health food breakfast place on the avenue." I described the rest of the case to him.

"Yet and still," he said, "you've got the wife. Two to one the wife offed him."

"She's a strange woman—about twenty years younger than him. Beautiful—thin, blond, aristocratic, every hair in place. She came out here for no decently explained reason. Before that she worked as an actresses in New York, but she can't remember the name of her longest-running play."

"Actress, huh? Actresses can take in a lot. Did the lady say she was acting on the stage or on the sheets?"

"She didn't say at all. But any actress I've met could tell you every role she'd ever had, and probably every line she spoke. The only job Mrs. Palmerston could remember was at Bloomingdale's."

"Maybe she had a rich daddy."

"She went to college on a scholarship."

"So what you're saying, Smith, is she had no money, she didn't make no money, she didn't bring no money with her, and then—Wham!—she buys a Mercedes and moves to Pacific Heights. If she's not peddling ass, then you spell that c-o-c-a-i-n-e, with a capital D for dealing."

"Could be. I guess I'm going to have to contact NYPD to see what they know."

"Don't hold your breath, Smith."

"Right. It won't be a high priority for them."

Jackson leaned back in the chair. It lurched. Jackson jerked forward, and laughed. "This sure is Howard's chair; like a man's favorite dog, it don't suit no one else."

I nodded. Jackson's strength was in his chest. Howard's was in his long legs. No one swivel chair could accommodate them both. "The thing is, Clay, there are all these—not even loose ends—strands that don't come anywhere near each other. There's Lois Palmerston. Maybe she was a call girl. Maybe she was dealing. Either one makes sense. But what does that have to do with her husband's brake lines being cut? From what her friends say, she freeloaded off them for years then dumped them as soon as she'd bagged money. Not pleasant, but not unheard of. Friends don't kill over that. And then there's Shareholders Five—a group that Palmerston hired Herman Ott to investigate so he could do something nice for each member."

Jackson snorted. "Nice, huh?"

I shrugged. "I quote Ott."

"Nice doesn't usually come before murder. Nice doesn't go with Herman Ott."

"Yeah, well . . ."

"You say this guy Palmerston's been involved with charity for years? You'd think he would know how to be nice without paying Herman Ott to tell him."

"In any case he didn't do anything good for Adam

Thede. And whoever the other four Shareholders are, Herman Ott's not about to tell me."

Now it was Jackson's turn to nod. "Then you're not going to find out, not from him. I've held off three guys with knives in an alley, but I've never gotten Ott to tell me anything he didn't have to."

"It just makes me so mad. He knows who those other four people are—he denies it, of course. Damn!"

"Yet and still, Smith, you've got the wife. You got a lot to dig around with there." He stood up, pointedly looking at his watch. It was quarter to two.

I watched him walk out, then looked down at my closed note pad. I considered reviewing my notes, but the interviews had been only this morning. Instead, I wrote out the request for anything NYPD had on Lois Burk, now Lois Palmerston. Then I called information and got the number for Binghamton College, Lois's alma mater. It was ten to two, ten to five Eastern time. The financial aid office staff should still be in.

I deliberated briefly whether to try a subterfuge. Bureaucrats, even in little bureaucracies, are not anxious to give information to the police. But no one other than a police officer or a bill collector would have called a college for the facts I needed.

I was put on hold twice, but at the end of that wait, a voice—clearly an old voice—came on.

"Miss Lowell here. May I help you?"

"I'm from the Berkeley, California, police. I need some information about one of your former scholarship students."

"All our students are treated alike. Money makes no difference."

"It's the repayment of the scholarship I'm interested in. The woman I just spoke to—"

"Miss Grimes."

"Miss Grimes said you were in charge of those records."

"Have been for thirty years."

"Wonderful. You must know every scholarship student."

"I do. But I can't give out information about them. Our records are confidential."

Damn. "I'm sure. And I wouldn't ask you to violate your regulations. I *am* a police officer; I'm sworn to uphold the law. I just wanted to know if you recognized the name Lois Burk?"

There was a long pause. I could picture a gray-haired lady pressing her lips together.

"I'm not asking you if she was on scholarship. I know she was."

I could hear her breathing.

"She graduated twelve years ago," I prompted.

Her breath was sharper.

"Students on scholarship, full scholarship, are also expected to work and to carry loans, right? You can tell me that."

"Yes," she snapped.

"And repayment is to begin a year after the student leaves college?"

When she didn't reply, I said, "This is just general information I'm asking for."

Her breath was shorter. "Yes," she snapped again. "We give them a whole year after their final semester of college, whether that be a bachelor's or a master's degree, or a doctorate. They have an entire year before they have to pay one cent."

"And some of them don't pay?"

"No, they don't. They take our money with open hands, but when it comes to paying it back, that's another story, I can tell you."

"And there's not much way of forcing them, is there?"

"We write to them, remind them of their responsibility, tell them that there are students who need that money, but they don't care. They've gotten what they need, they don't think about those who come after them."

"Of course, there are collection agencies . . . ?" I left the question open, pleased that I had been able to tap into her outrage.

"For a long time the board didn't want to stoop to collection agencies. They didn't like to think our students were the kind to be badgered by bill collectors. But when I showed the board the financial statement, even they saw that there was very little difference between some of our fine upwardly mobile graduates, and deadbeats."

"I'll bet the collection agencies have gotten some action."

"They've brought in more money than our nice letters did."

"But even they can't get everyone to pay."

"No. Some they can't find. Some don't have anything. And some of them—would you believe this?—they quit perfectly good jobs rather than pay their debts. Of course, if there's nothing to attach, there's no way of getting them. But we keep checking. They can't stay out of work forever. Sooner or later they'll take a job where they keep records. And then we get them."

I could almost see her pouncing. "And Lois Burk?" I held my breath.

"Never paid one cent. Never had a job long enough to attach her wages. I remember that girl. I remember her in here crying that she needed another scholarship, a bigger loan. She stood right here in this office and told me how she was going to New York and get herself a good job so she could pay back our generosity. They tell me she was an actress. I can tell you she was a good one. Not one cent."

13

Detective Inspector Doyle's office was in the rear corner of the Detective Division, behind the protection of the division secretary. At two o'clock I walked to her desk and she motioned me on.

Doyle's office was not much larger than mine and Howard's. Rank could only do so much. But instead of our slatted excuse for a window, he had a large, old-fashioned, wood-framed window that gave him not only the morning sun (on those days when the fog lifted before eleven) but a rear view of the colonnaded school adminis-tration building. Compared to Lois Palmerston's view, it was not much, but stacked up against the other possibili-ties in this building, it was big stuff.

Note pad in hand, I sat on the straight-backed wooden chair he indicated. While a beat officer, I had had plenty of interviews with Lieutenant Davis. In each, I'd come ready to explain not so much my thinking about a case, as what steps I had taken, what information I'd found out. And Lieutenant Davis had sat behind his orderly desk, occasionally straightening an already geometric pile of papers, his feelings veiled behind his caramel-colored face. I had learned not to commit myself too soon; I'd learned to be more thorough than I liked; and over those years I'd picked up those subtle signals that were open-ings for discussion.

But now, seated next to a desk that bore a closer resemblance to my closet floor than Lieutenant Davis's desk, I found all my old markers useless.

Inspector Doyle leaned back in his chair, awkwardly feeling for the armrests with his elbows. He was a tall man and at one time he had weighed more than 250 pounds. But now most of the excess was gone. The rumor was that he was going in for a series of medical tests. His prognosis, as assembled by the rumor mill, didn't look hopeful. And his appearance did nothing to belie that speculation. He looked deflated; his uniform hung; his normally florid skin drooped. The bags under his eyes rested on his cheekbones. Even his eyebrows drooped almost into his eyes. And his hair, which had once been as fiery as Howard's, was now muted with gray.

With an effort, he pushed a pile of papers to the side and leaned forward. "Smith, you're new in this detail. This is your first homicide."

"I had others when I was a patrol officer."

He nodded. His flesh rolled with the movement. "The, uh, Palmerston case has been assigned to you since, when, this morning?"

"Yessir."

"Not much time."

"No sir."

"Normally I wouldn't have you in to discuss it yet. Probably not for another twenty-four hours."

I waited.

He shifted his weight to one elbow. "I'm going to be straight with you, Smith. You're the first woman we've had here. The department supports equal opportunities. Our record's as good if not better than any department in the state. But I have to tell you, I had some questions about a woman detective in Homicide. Press Officer, sure. Special Investigations, dangerous but effective. But Homicide . . ."

I could feel my lips pressing together in anger.

"But Lieutenant Davis pushed for you. I'll be honest, Smith, I didn't want to have a woman who was too soft, who got too emotionally involved with the widows, who didn't want to ask the tough questions—"

"Inspector, I—"

"Let me finish, Smith. Like I said, I had my reservations. But what I didn't expect was that when you'd been on the case for less than one day, there would be a complaint about you."

I stared.

"Police harassment."

"What? From whom?"

"One of the city council members called at noon. Had a complaint that you were badgering the widow."

"Badgering! Jesus! I waited till eleven o'clock this morning so I wouldn't wake her up. Then the woman wouldn't even let me in the house. I was trying to be considerate. Look, I broke the news to her last night—on my own time. It wasn't even my case yet. I was just assisting Pereira then. I drove her to the morgue—on my own time. I offered to stay with her until she could have a friend come. How much less badgering can you do? If she hadn't complained, you'd be saying I was too soft with her."

Doyle sighed. "The problem is, Smith, that the woman's got connections."

"There are things I need to see in that house, things she could be destroying right now. I wouldn't put money on her innocence."

"Calm down, Smith. Half of being a cop is diplomacy."

I took a breath. "Sir, when Ralph Palmerston's car left the Cadillac dealership yesterday afternoon it was certified in perfect shape."

"Smith—"

"Sir, if you'll let me explain."

Grudgingly, he nodded.

"Palmerston left there and drove straight home. And at some point between the time he got home and the time he left, his brake lines were cut."

"You think the wife could have cut the brake lines?"

I had my own reservations about Lois Palmerston under a car, but it galled me to admit that now. "If it means you'll inherit a fortune, it's something you can learn."

He slumped back in his chair, his hand automatically going to rest on the paunch that was no more and landing on his leg. "I see what you're saying, Smith. I'm not questioning your suspicions. But unfortunately, that doesn't alter the fact that you're going to have to tread carefully. This is not a case that will go unnoticed. So far the papers have only reported it as an accident. But it won't take them long to see a Homicide officer asking questions and to put two and two together. Then it's going to be front-page news. They'll be asking why we don't have a suspect in custody, why we're dragging our feet. The last thing we need is for them to add that instead of tracking down the killer, the detective in charge is out browbeating the widow. You follow, Smith?"

"Yessir. But I need to get in the house. Maybe a warrant?"

"Holy Mother! Smith, it's bad enough they're complaining about you harassing, how do you think a warrant would go down?"

"But, sir—"

"Smith, I know it's frustrating. You've got to walk a fine line. You let this case go unsolved too long and the people in the hills will be screaming that we don't bother with murder unless the corpse was dealing coke. You push this woman and she'll have a lawyer raising hell. But, Smith, this is the type of thing that Lieutenant Davis told me you could handle. It's what got you the nod for this job."

And, I thought, failing at this is exactly what will plunk me back to patrol officer. "Sir," I said, "I've been

assuming Lois Palmerston called in the complaint herself. Is that right?"

He shrugged. "No way to know. By law the council
members don't have to reveal the source of their complaints. And they don't."

It was clear the interview was over. I stood up, nodded, and opened the door. I nearly smacked into the
chief. In formal departments, the chief would have called
Inspector Doyle into his office, but Berkeley was more
relaxed. If Chief Larkin wanted something, he had no
qualms about walking down the hall. He stood outside
the door in his gray suit and narrow red tie—another
informality. When I had started on the force, I had assumed the chief would wear a uniform. He had one, I
found out, but we didn't see it often. A well-tailored suit,
he had once said, was his uniform. But in truth, it was
the tie that was his personal badge of office. Years passed,
styles changed, thin ties gave way to wide splashily flowered ones. But for Chief Larkin, the narrow red tie was
constant.

As he nodded at me, his expression revealed nothing,
though I knew, as chief, he had gotten word of the complaint.

When I got back to my office, Howard was in his chair
and Pereira was on his desk, her feet propped on his open
bottom drawer.

"Well?" Howard asked.

"News gets around fast," I said, sitting in my own
chair. "Almost as fast as you get back from Leon Evans's
place. I thought you'd be gone for hours."

"Finished early," he said with a shrug.

"About your meeting with Doyle," Pereira said.
"What happened? He doesn't usually focus in on a case
this soon, or so they tell me."

"Most cases don't have a harassment complaint before
the day is out."

"What?" they said together.

"Complaint that I badgered the widow."

"I was kidding about you billy-clubbing prisoners to let off steam," Howard said.

I shrugged off Howard's attempt to lighten the atmosphere. To Pereira I said, "What have you found out this morning?"

"Other than Lois Palmerston's one mention in the society column for giving a breakfast party, not much. I left you a note about the accountant."

"Right. Anything more than you said there?"

"Not really, and I know he told me all there is. I started off by mentioning my drink with Paul Lucas and name-dropped along for a few minutes. Gorley, the accountant, was impressed. He should have been. The names I tossed out were the royal family of West Coast finances—much too far above his level for him to check on me."

"Did he know anything about Lois Palmerston's money before her marriage?"

"If she had any, it was below the level of his attention. You know, Jill, to those people less than a hundred thousand is called a nuisance account."

"What I had in mind was the difference between Lois arriving with nothing or with five thousand."

Pereira shook her head. "To Gorley, a pauper is a pauper."

"What about the lawyer?"

"John Farrell? He's completely reliable. His firm is known for representing money. They handled Palmerston's father's affairs. And I can tell you it wasn't easy to get anything out of him."

"What did you?"

"Probably nothing you don't already know. After he got the okay from the widow, he told me that she gets everything. No strings attached."

"What did he say about Palmerston himself?"

She laughed. "As little as possible, of course. But the

picture he painted was of an old-line conservative who felt it was his duty as a member of the gentry to do his part. It was a picture Farrell approved of."

"How come this guy lived in Berkeley?" Howard demanded. "He could have lived down the Peninsula with the rest of the money."

Pereira smiled. "Actually, I know the answer to that too. Farrell found it odd—well, appalling is more accurate. He said, of course Palmerston didn't enjoy the 'radical atmosphere of lunacy'—that's a quote. But he liked the weather, he carried on about his view, and he had his house fitted out to suit him."

I recalled Palmerston's panoramic view. His attachment to it made me think fondly of him. "I'm beginning to wonder what is going on with Lois Palmerston. Here she is giving her attorney permission to tell us about her husband's will, being as helpful as she can, and the next thing she files a complaint about me. Maybe Jackson was right. Maybe she had a shady past. She could have been a call girl in San Francisco. She could be trying to keep me from asking about that."

"I can check for you," Howard said. "I am in Special Investigations now. Vice and drugs are my bread and butter. If SFPD had made a collar, we'd know. But I can call over there and find out if there were any suspicions about her. Someone may recognize the name."

"But Jill," Periera said, "are you sure *she* was the one complaining about you?"

"Well, no. But who else would care? Who else would *know?*"

Pereira shifted her feet on the desk drawer.

Howard asked, "If you don't see her for a while, what happens?"

"Or what doesn't happen?"

"Well, the main thing is that I don't get to search the house, and I don't get a look at Herman Ott's report to

Palmerston on Shareholders Five, assuming Palmerston kept that in the house."

"He probably did," Pereira said.

I stared at her.

"Farrell," she said quickly. "He complained that Palmerston tended to keep important papers at home as long as he thought he might have to refer to them—long after Farrell felt they should have been in his safe deposit box."

"Well, wherever he kept it, I'm not likely to see it."

"So then, who is it who benefits by your not seeing it?" Howard asked. He leaned back in his chair thoughtfully, stretching his legs across the room. "Lois Palmerston?"

"I don't know. I asked her about Shareholders Five and she had no reaction. It could be that it has nothing to do with her."

"The Shareholders themselves," Pereira suggested.

"Possibly, but according to Adam Thede, he didn't know anything about being chosen for Palmerston's beneficence."

"You believe that?" Howard asked.

"I'm letting that decision ride. But even if Thede is lying and he knows he's part of the group, that doesn't mean he knows that Palmerston hired a detective to check on them. What Herman Ott told Palmerston he could have figured out himself. So—" I laughed.

"What?"

"One person who gains by keeping that report a secret is Herman Ott. I told him that with his client dead no one but us would pay for his research. He gave me a scrap of it, but hardly twenty pages' worth."

Howard rolled forward. "So ol' Herman Ott's sitting on his perch waiting to sell you Palmerston's information bit by bit."

"Unless," Pereira added, "you can get to that report first, in which case Ott gets nothing."

"Nothing beyond what Palmerston paid him, which

was probably more than his normal fees," I said. I stood up, stuffing my note pad in my pocket.

As I reached for the door, Howard said, "Now don't you go harassing Herman Ott."

14

I signed out a Homicide black and white and drove to Telegraph, leaving it in the red zone in front of Ott's building. The sun was bright, the air still post-storm fresh. Telegraph Avenue looked just cleaned. The rain had washed the pizza papers and dog turds off the sidewalk. Many people complained that the avenue they knew was disappearing in a wave of gentrification. New boutiques and croissant shops boasted bright tile, clean windows, and orange neon signs. They gave the impression that the entire avenue could be hosed clean. Next to them, Ott's building looked older, grimier, and more squalid.

I charged up the exterior staircase between buildings. The door was propped open. It was after school hours and the second-floor hallway looked like a playground with a mixture of the children of the avenue regulars and those of refugee families.

The third-floor hallway contained a drunk who had keeled over from a sitting position and was now sprawled on the floor. I stepped around him and banged on Ott's door.

"Who's there?"

"Smith, Homicide." Already I was shouting.

He pulled the door open.

I barged in past him. "What do you mean calling in a complaint about this case?"

He moved back around his desk. "Hey, hold it, what are you talking about?"

"Look, don't stall. We had an arrangement. The department was going to pay you for work that you've already collected on once. And then you call a city council member and put in a harassment charge."

Ott stared across at me, his yellow-clad shoulders hunched. "Come on, Smith, everyone knows I don't like the cops. What council member is going to take my complaint seriously? I wouldn't waste my time."

I pushed the door shut and stepped closer to the desk. "There's a new city council, Ott. The liberals are out; the radical slate is in. They like us even less than the old group did. Nothing is so Establishment as the police department. They're just beginning their terms. Some of them would be delighted to hear a complaint, even from you. Some of those new members," I said more slowly, "might not even know who you are."

"They know." He glanced tentatively at the city directory on his desk. "Much as it is against my principals to give the cops any free information, I'll tell you this, Smith. I didn't make any complaint."

"Why should I believe that?"

He shrugged. The yellow sweater settled stiffly back on his shoulders. "Believe what you want. But I have to use the council members from time to time. It's good business for me to be on the up-and-up with them. They're only going to do so much for me, so I have to—say—ration my requests."

That made sense. "Still, by my not getting into Palmerston's house, I don't see your report and the one person who stands to gain, financially, by that is you."

He nodded.

"You can go a long way toward making me believe you

didn't file that complaint by neutralizing the effect. You can tell me what's in that report."

He shook his head in disbelief. "Smith, you attach a high price to your belief. Why should I care what you think I did?"

I smiled. I'd hit on one of the strands of Ott's ethical underpinnings, like his embarrassment at having given Ralph Palmerston information he could have found himself. "I know you've got more than just one name of the Shareholders Five. You turned in that report. You hit on exactly what was important to Adam Thede. There was no reason Palmerston wouldn't have been pleased with your work."

A small smile flickered on Ott's face.

"So there was also no reason he wouldn't have given you the rest of the names. And since he must have paid you a lot more than your regular clients, you wouldn't hold off getting to them."

"I'm not saying anything. I know my rights."

"Give me one name. With one name it won't matter that I can't get to your report. It will"—I searched for the right word—"underline the integrity of our agreement."

He leaned back against the file cabinet. "I already gave you one name, Smith. I haven't seen any money."

"It's been less than twenty-four hours. You're dealing with government. You don't get your tax refund for months." When he didn't say anything, I added, "I've done my half."

He seemed to shrink back in thought. He looked like nothing so much as a canary with a big furry cat under its cage.

"On one condition, Smith. And I mean this. You break your word on this and we never do business again, on anything."

"What?"

"You don't admit to anyone where you got this from. Ever."

"Okay," I said, relieved. "You've got my word."

Looking over my shoulder, he said, "Carol Grogan."

"Carol Grogan!" I said in amazement. "Lois Palmerston's friend."

"I'm not saying another word, Smith. Out."

I didn't press. I'd already gotten much more than I could have hoped for. I almost thanked him, but to Herman Ott thanks from a cop would have been an insult.

Carol Grogan, I thought as I made my way down the stairs, was the woman Lois Palmerston had had dinner with last night, the woman who had left her alone while she went to pick up her children from day care. Swenson, the officer on her beat, had checked on that. But it was time I saw her myself. I looked at my watch. Ten to four. Plenty of time.

I stood for a moment on the sidewalk. The sun was getting low. Shadows hung almost to the middle of the street. Sidewalk sellers of leather pouches and belts were gathering up their wares and folding the blankets they had been on. Ott had told me another thing besides Carol Grogan's name. He'd given me good reason to believe he hadn't been the complainant. But if not him, then who? Lois Palmerston stood out. With Ott's information, I could file that question away for later. I turned toward the car.

"Hello there."

Startled, I looked up at the languid, handsome face.

"Cap Danziger," he said, extending a hand. "It was my Cadillac showroom you chose to dry off in last night." He wore jeans and a French blue turtleneck that accentuated his silver-blue eyes. A gray corduroy jacket hung over his arm. All of them—the jeans, the turtleneck, and the jacket—looked carefully chosen and expensive. He looked about as different from Herman Ott as one was likely to get. When he smiled—an easy, confident smile, again at the far end of the spectrum from Ott's wary-of-the-cat look—even his teeth gleamed.

"Are you getting ready to go on duty?"

"No." It took me a minute to realize that since he had seen me yesterday in the evening, he would think that that was my shift. "No, actually, I work days. Like a normal person."

"Must be nice. I wish people could be forced by law to buy cars between nine and five. Could you do that for me?"

"I don't have the power now. Wait till I'm chief." I was anxious to get to Carol Grogan's, excited about my discovery. But Cap Danziger was a very attractive man. A couple of minutes wouldn't hurt.

"I was going to suggest I walk you to your car, but I suppose that's it by the curb."

" 'Fraid so."

"Well then, how about a drink after work, since you work such civilized hours?"

Again I hesitated. How long would Carol Grogan take? Then there were the reports to write up. I looked back at Danziger's silver-blue eyes, the easy half-smile as he watched the man who sold cloisonné earrings packing up. "Sometimes my work runs over. Could we make it later?"

"Let's say eight. Then we'll have the evening."

"Okay."

"Make it even easier, since you know where the showroom is, why don't you come by? Then if you're late, you won't have to worry. It will just mean that I've sold another de Ville."

"Great," I said, opening the squad car door. I slid under the wheel. Cap Danziger reached toward the door, then drew his hand back, as if realizing he shouldn't help a cop shut her door.

I sat for a moment, checking my note pad for Carol Grogan's address. It was across town in North Berkeley,

not far from where I lived. As I pulled into traffic, I
found myself uneasy. It might have been from anticipation of confronting Carol Grogan and maybe finding the
key to Shareholders Five, but I didn't think so. The answer was a little closer. Cap Danziger was a very appealing man. There was something about him, about his very
blue eyes, about the way the turtleneck hung off shoulders that were wide but not overmuscular; about his
quickness and good sense in not closing the car door.
There was definitely something about this man that got
to me.

I turned left, driving past the University. It had been a
long time since I had felt this kind of intense attraction.
Had Nat, my ex-husband, elicited that? I couldn't remember. The early days with him, in college, when everything was exciting, had been overwhelmed by the
years after we moved to Berkeley. He had entered gradu-
ate school on his way to becoming a professor, and after
searching for the right job to fill the interval before we
moved on to some ivy-covered little college where he
would begin his climb up the academic ladder, I had
joined the force. From then it was just a question of
whether things were falling apart slowly or at slam-bang
pace. Our lives diverged. He agonized over the Oriental
influence in Yeats's poetry and I chased felons into alleys.
The give-and-take (more accurately, take-and-take) of
our divorce removed any veneer of maturity. Nat interrupted my work on a murder case because he didn't think
it was important. I sullied his dissertation notes because I
knew how vital they were to him.

And after that was over, I kept my distance from men.
No romances at work—that was an unbreakable rule. No
flirtations with suspects or victims, or those likely to be—
only common sense. I had never broken those rules. The
only time I'd even been tempted was when Howard and I
were out drinking one night. And even then I'd pulled

back. Howard was my friend, probably my closest friend, and I wasn't about to endanger that.

I had protected myself so well, that now what must have seemed like a normal reaction to the average woman came as a surprise. But Cap Danziger didn't break any of my rules.

I screeched to a halt as students raced into the cross-walk. I decided I'd better think about Cap Danziger when I wasn't driving.

15

I climbed up the four wooden steps to Carol Grogan's door and rang the bell. Carol Grogan worked at the Albany library. After State Proposition 13 had cut funds to local governments, the library had limited its hours. Some days it opened at ten, others at two and stayed open through the evening. Today it was closed all day.

The woman who answered the doorbell was about my height, five foot seven, with shoulder-length brown hair that was streaked with just enough gray to make it noticeable. She wore a royal blue T-shirt that said READ and brown sweatpants over hips that had sat too long in a chair. Her eyes were brown and set wide apart, her nose thin until the end, when it spread abruptly to the sides, as if to balance her eyes. Her skin had that same pallid coloring as Herman Ott's. She looked as if she had been cleaning house. But the room behind her was clearly not what she'd been working on. She looked tired and irritated, but her face held the promise that with rest, sun, and makeup she could use those unusual features to make herself striking. Now they were drawn down into a scowl.

"I'm Detective Smith, Berkeley Police." I held out my shield. "Are you Carol Grogan?"

"Yes," she said with the normal wariness.

"I'd like to talk to you about Ralph Palmerston."

She hesitated, glancing behind her at the living room
that was littered with push trucks and plastic cars, small
polo shirts, a beach ball, a red rubber football, and a
virtual hurricane of small plastic building blocks in various bright plastic colors. "Come on in, if you can find
your way. I was babysitting a two- and four-year-old this
morning. I should forget that and enroll them in
janitorial training."

I stepped over what appeared to be two concentric
plastic circles with a handle on top. Seeing my confusion,
she said, "It spins, but you have to be under five to figure
out how to use it."

Pushing aside a Richard Scarry book with trains and
cars and other odd vehicles on the cover, I sat on the
couch. Carol Grogan cleaned off an ottoman opposite. I
was just about to speak when the phone rang.

"Excuse me."

"Sure."

She walked through the dining room to the kitchen to
take the call. The house was typical of Berkeley, with the
living room across the front, the dining room and kitchen
in line behind it, and a door leading from the dining room
into a square hallway that in turn led to both bedrooms
and the bathroom in between. In contrast to the jumble
of the living room, the dining room was an adult area. An
antique cherry table and sideboard stood on an Oriental
rug. In the built-in cabinet was a set of gilt-edged china.
The furniture dwarfed the room, as if it had come from a
larger house, from a wealthier life style that Carol Grogan was not willing to let go of.

"Sorry," she said, settling back on the ottoman. "That
was one of my research people wanting to know the ex-
tent of Julia Morgan's influence on architecture in the
East Bay. I needed to get some specifics."

"Is that how you know Lois Palmerston, through architecture?" I asked, remembering that Lois had worked
for an architectural firm.

She stared a moment, then shook her head. "No. I'm not a specialist in architecture. I do research. This client just happens to be into Julia Morgan."

"Is that part of your job at the library?"

"No. It's a side business. A very small side business. I am a conglomerate of Carol Grogan Research, Carol Grogan Typing Services, and more often than I'd like, Carol Grogan Babysitting. My job at the library is only part-time. The payments on this house alone cost a fortune. And my kids go through clothes like they were an EPA testing service."

"Their father—"

"Their father," she said with a sigh of disgust, "was in middle management with an oil company. When we were married, we bought a house at the base of the hills. It seemed like we were paying a fortune then. Now that house costs twice as much as this, and I can't afford either. What you were going to ask was, do I get support from him, right?" She didn't wait for an answer. "I did for a while. When we were married, he traveled. He said he hated to be away. Then, after a while, he stopped saying that. Then he stopped coming home. And lately he's stopped paying support."

"There are laws."

"Yeah. After he stopped paying, he also stopped working. He said he was setting up his own business, something to do with arranging to supply oil to small companies on an emergency basis. It sounded to me like shipping a couple gallons to Sioux Falls when they had a blizzard. But whatever it is, or was, it's not making money. I could take him to court, but there's nothing to get. So I type, research, and watch kids."

"What I wanted to ask you," I said, "was about Ralph and Lois Palmerston. You had dinner with her last night."

"When he was murdered," she said.

"Did Lois call and tell you that?"

"I saw it on the two o'clock news this afternoon."

So the press had realized it was murder. I'd hoped it would take them longer.

"Did you call her then?"

"No. I figured she would either be sedated, or in the morgue, or whatever she was doing she wouldn't want people calling up."

This was beginning to sound like the Munsons' comments. I asked, "Would you say you were a close friend of Lois's?"

"Oh, no. Not now. We were friendly only a short time, when my boys were little. That'd be five years ago. But our lives are hardly the same now. I wouldn't expect Lois Palmerston to endure this"—she motioned around the room—"any too often."

"But you did invite her to dinner last night."

"Yesterday was a good day. I had the day off. I could go to the store, I could cook." She picked up a polo shirt and began folding it, though it was obviously stained. "It was a lark, the invitation. Or maybe lark is too cheerful a word. You see, Lois and I had this brief and rather odd friendship. We met at the movies. My husband was in Saudi. And I had this rather embarrassing passion for Peter O'Toole. The UC Theater was having a Peter O'Toole festival. I began to notice Lois there a couple of days. You do that. There's sort of a conspiracy feeling. And then when she sat through two showings of *The Ruling Class,* I knew we were meant to be friends." She picked up a handful of plastic building blocks and began stacking them, sticking the protrusions of one into the holes of the next. "It was odd though, or maybe not, but our friendship didn't go much beyond Peter O'Toole. It wasn't like we had a similar streak of adolescence. It was just one small matching blotch. And after a while we'd said all we could about him. I mean, how much can a stranger, even a famous stranger, fill out conversation.

And I didn't care about his life. I only loved his eyes and his chest."

"But you did invite Lois Palmerston to dinner."

"Yes."

"Because . . . ?"

"Well . . . okay. I wanted to borrow money. I knew she'd married a really rich man."

"What did she say?"

"Nothing."

"Nothing?"

"I never asked. It was clear five minutes after she got here that there was no point. To say we had nothing in common is suggesting a closeness that wasn't there." She smiled briefly. "I'll bet that was the first meal she'd had with a six-year-old demanding honey on his garlic bread and a seven-year-old critiquing each entrée with 'Gross!' She probably isn't used to banging into a bicycle when she pushes her chair back either."

Remembering Lois Palmerston in her silk pants and sweater, I could understand Carol Grogan's assessment. "She stayed here by herself before dinner when you went to pick up the children." I left the "that seems strange" unspoken.

"This time of year, half the kids are coming down with the flu. I figured she didn't need to be exposed. People without kids don't have the immunities we do. And besides, it didn't take a genius to see Lois wouldn't enjoy the day-care scene. Lois didn't have to put up with that. I guess those are the joys of wealth."

Or childlessness, I thought. "Why didn't you ask Ralph Palmerston for the money?"

"Ralph? I never met the man. He would have had no more reason to make a loan to me than he would to you."

"What about Shareholders Five?"

Her dark eyes opened wide. "I don't know what you're talking about."

"Mrs. Grogan, you were one of a group of five people

that Ralph Palmerston made a point to find out about. He went to a lot of trouble to discover what was important to you."

"He did? What did he find out?"

"You tell me."

"How would I know?"

"If someone were investigating you for that reason, what would they come up with?"

"Dustin and Jason, my kids, I guess."

"Has anything changed with them in the past two weeks or so? Have they gotten any gifts, or been accepted at a better school or"—I was in deep water here trying to think what a philanthropist could do for a six- and seven-year-old or what a misanthrope could do to distress them —"or have they been denied gymnastics classes?"

"No, they still spend the day in school and day care and come home refreshed and ready to empty their closets all over the living room floor."

"What about your job?"

"At the library? It's civil service. Unless the county comes up with more money, I'm not likely to get longer hours or, God forbid, a raise. Prop. Thirteen will keep me in poverty till the boys are in college."

There was only one other possibility. "This is your house, right?"

"Mine and the bank's." Her eyes widened again.

"Has anything changed with it—the payments, the insurance? Has anyone made you an offer to buy it?"

"No." Her reply was too quick.

"Look, this is very serious. You have young children. You have a lot of responsibilities. You don't have time to get entangled on the wrong side of a murder investigation. Now, I know something important in your life has changed. What is it?"

She eyed a handful of plastic blocks but didn't reach for them. "Nothing's changed. The kids are the same. We live in the same place. I do the same work. Their father still doesn't pay support."

"Have you heard from their father in the last two weeks?"

"No."

I leaned forward. "You say you were barely friends with Lois Palmerston five years ago. Then, all of a sudden, you call her. She comes to dinner and that night her husband is murdered. Now we find you were one of the five people he was investigating. And you're telling me that you don't know him and nothing's changed in your life. I don't believe that for a minute. Either you can give me a truthful answer or you can have me leave here wondering what it is you're hiding. And you can have me and the officers working under me make it a priority to find out."

Now she did grab a handful of the tiny blocks.

"Mrs. Grogan?"

"I've told you everything. I'm amazed Ralph Palmerston was checking on me. I'm outraged." She sounded not outraged but nervous. "He wouldn't have known me on the street. What business was it of his how I spent my money?"

How I spent my money. "You were going to ask Lois for a loan. What for?"

She pushed the plastic blocks one into the next, forming a line. "You know, Christmas. The kids."

I forced myself to control my anger. I didn't need another complaint. "Mrs. Grogan, you don't call a casual friend you haven't seen in years, a woman with no interest in children, to borrow money for presents for boys who already have plenty."

She stared down at the blocks.

"We'll check your finances. We'll go to your bank, to the mortgage company, to the library, the county offices. Do you want that?" When she didn't reply, I said, "Do you?"

"Okay, okay. It's the second mortgage. I'm behind. I thought it was no problem. It was held by a man in the Oakland hills. He'd always been very nice about it. Then, suddenly, he said he needed money and demanded all the back payments."

"How much?"

"Four months. Three hundred and fifty each. Fourteen hundred. I just didn't have that. I wasn't sure I could get it. But, I thought, to Lois fourteen hundred dollars was nothing. She must have coats that are worth more than that."

"But you didn't ask her for the money. Now what are you going to do?"

"I don't know. I'm trying to get in touch with Mr. Hargis. I've left messages. I don't know."

I asked her for Mr. Hargis's address and phone number. She knew them by memory. Extricating a toy car from between the sofa cushions, I said, "Tell me about Adam Thede."

"Adam Thede? The name doesn't sound familiar."

"You and he are lumped together in this investigation."

"How? In what?"

"It doesn't matter. What I want to find out is how you know him."

She looked down at the pile of blocks on her lap, as if she was surprised to see them all separated. "I *don't* know him."

"Think."

She sat for a moment, but I doubted she was searching her memory. "I suppose I could have met him at a party. You meet a lot of people like that and you don't recall their names later."

"How else?"

"At the library."

"How is it, Mrs. Grogan, that Ralph Palmerston would consider you two in the same light?"

"I don't know. I was a very casual friend of Lois's. Maybe this Thede was too. But surely Lois must have had more than five friends of that caliber."

"What about Nina and Jeffrey Munson?"

"No. I don't know them either."

"Lois lived with them when you knew her."

"That could be, but I wouldn't have met them unless they came to the movies."

I stood up. "Mrs. Grogan, you are at the center of this murder investigation. You are the only person who was pinpointed both by Ralph Palmerston and a friend of Lois's. I know there's something you're not telling me. I don't want to have to spend a lot of my time finding that out. Now, here's my card. It has my office number and my home number. Call me when you decide that it's more sensible to be completely honest with the police."

She didn't say anything. She didn't even look up. Stepping over a fire engine, I walked out.

I got into the car and headed to lower Marin Avenue. I'd been tough with Carol Grogan. She was holding something back; I didn't know how much. But she had also given me a new slant on the case. Carol Grogan and her second mortgage. As soon as I could talk to Mr. Hargis, I'd have a clearer idea of exactly how Ralph Palmerston was operating with the information Herman Ott had gotten him.

It was after five o'clock. I should have gone back to the station and started dictating all my day's interviews. They had to be on Inspector Doyle's desk before Detectives' Morning Meeting. But I had a squad car. I could get up the hill fast. I could tackle—very gently—Lois Palmerston.

16

It was dusk. Some cars had their headlights on. Lamps shone through curtains in living room windows. But the Palmerston house was dark. With the garage door closed it wasn't possible to tell whether Lois was out or just hadn't put the lights on. I rang the bell by the gate and waited.

There was no answer. No head peered over the wooden shutters in the living room. I rang again.

Behind me a door slammed. I turned. "Oh, Billy, hi."

Billy Kershon, half running, half walking, arrived at my side. He stood, shifting his weight from one gangly leg to the other. "Hi. I don't think she's there. I mean, I haven't seen her all day."

"Didn't you go to school?"

"Oh, yeah, that. Well, I mean when I was here."

"I guess you didn't get sick, then."

"Nah. Ma sees germs everywhere. It's like this humungous conspiracy of germs all aimed at me, you know?"

I smiled. With the coming of dusk the afternoon winds had picked up. It was chilly, but as if to flaunt his health against the invisible army of microbes, Billy Kershon wore a T-shirt and shorts. "Is there something you wanted to tell me?"

"No. I just wanted to know how things were going."

I glanced back at the Palmerston house. There was still no movement there. "They're going okay," I said, "but if you know anything, tell me. I can use all the help I can get. Later, after this case is over and we're not so rushed in Homicide, why don't you come down to the station and I can show you around?"

"Really? You mean not just the ride-along with the guys on the beat, but Homicide?"

"Right."

"Great."

"Listen, you better get back inside before your mother sees you out here in shorts."

"Yeah, I know. Germs." He hesitated and then turned and loped across the street.

I gave a final look to the Palmerston house. Nothing had changed. I felt uneasy about leaving. Lois Palmerston hadn't been in good condition when I'd seen her last. If she was in there now, who knew what shape she'd be in. But there was nothing I could do. Or at least nothing more than leaving my card with a note to call me at work or at home if she was ready to talk. I made a show of slipping it through the mail shoot into the box inside the courtyard wall. If Lois was in the house watching, she would see me.

I drove down Marin, adolescently enjoying the firm hold of the squad car brakes. At the traffic circle where Ralph Palmerston had been killed, cars shot out from all six entry roads. It was a game of chicken. Again adolescently, I bullied my way in. For a Volkswagen driver, used to anything bigger than a Honda cutting me off, being behind the wheel of a black and white was heaven.

As soon as I was at my desk, I called Hargis. He had held Carol Grogan's second mortgage, but he'd sold it three weeks ago. Had he, I asked, called in payment before then? With that question, Hargis got cagey. He had told me enough. Part of the deal of selling it—he'd gotten a good price, a damned good price—was that he say

nothing about it. And he intended to keep his word. I
asked if he'd sold it to Ralph Palmerston. Again, he said
he couldn't tell me anything, but the pause before his
reply was answer enough.

Then I turned my attention to my reports. Note pad in
hand, I headed for the dictating booths. It took longer
than I had expected. Frequently, the act of putting my
observations into sentence form served to clarify them
and illuminate an internal order that hadn't been clear to
me as I pondered them. But tonight, as I dictated my
interviews with Adam Thede, Jeffrey Munson, Nina
Munson, Lois Palmerston, and Carol Grogan, and an ed-
ited version of the two with Herman Ott, no one theme
emerged. There was Lois's opportunity to get to the
brake lines. There was Lois's shaky financial situation.
There was Lois's cutting off the friends she had depended
on as soon as she married Ralph. But there was also the
question of the Munsons and their reasons for helping
Lois. Had Nina Munson watched out for Lois all those
years and not cared when Lois dropped her?

And Jeffrey? I still wasn't willing to believe he hadn't
been attracted to Lois.

Shareholders Five? What did Adam Thede and Carol
Grogan have in common? And who were the other three
members? And what had drawn Ralph Palmerston's attention to them?

Those were the main disparate themes. For smaller
threads there were such questions as why Ralph Palmerston was so furious with Sam Nguyen at the repair shop?
Had Lois Palmerston been involved in prostitution or
with cocaine, as Jackson suggested? I wished I could
somehow braid them together. But what I had was just
separate hairs.

When I finished dictating, it was seven o'clock, much
later than I would have guessed.

I had thought of going home, taking a shower, putting
on fresh makeup before I met Cap Danziger. But it was

too late now. I hadn't eaten since the doughnuts this morning. I wasn't sure what, if anything, was in my fridge. And I was suddenly too ravenous to do without.

I straightened up my desk, and from habit checked my IN box—nothing that couldn't wait—and from new habit Howard's—nothing, period. I headed to Ay Caramba, the Mexican restaurant across University Avenue.

Ay Caramba was decorated like brightly colored Mexican pottery. A line of students waited to give their orders and take a plate of huevos rancheros (even at dinner) or tostada suprema to a table. It was already quarter after seven when I fell in behind two undergraduates in down jackets. "Governments believe what they want to believe," the tall one said.

The other—shorter, darker—nodded.

"Look at the Germans in World War Two. I mean, they decided to march through Belgium."

The shorter one nodded.

"Because they felt Belgium was rightfully theirs. And because they figured, as a matter of course, that all the other governments would understand that."

The companion nodded.

"And when they slaughtered the Belgians, they figured everyone would understand because they—the Belgians, I mean—shouldn't have been preventing the Germans from reclaiming what was rightfully theirs. See?"

Again, the nod.

"Now you look at our government. They think . . ."

Their dishes were on the counter. The silent companion grabbed for his. I moved forward, and in less than a minute my own taco special was before me. I carried it and a Coke to a table by the window, emptied my tray, and sat down, stacking the tray atop a pile on the next table.

There was a gentle tap on the window.

I turned.

No one was there.

It took me a moment to realize that the tapping was raindrops. "Damn," I said aloud. Of course, I didn't have an umbrella. As far as I knew, rain hadn't even been forecast for today.

I took off my jacket and draped it over my shoulders. Picking up the taco, I watched the rain. My thoughts turned back to Carol Grogan, but I caught myself. No. I was off duty. I had to leave my work at work. The Palmerston case was important, but now that I was in Homicide every case would be important. If I allowed myself to become absorbed in them, I wouldn't have any life at all outside work.

Instead I thought of Howard. What could that man be planning to wear to his Halloween party? It had to be something significant, timely. Something to do with the city, with the year? Clayton Jackson and his wife were coming in their Raiders shirts *("Oakland* Raiders," Clay had explained, "not those L.A. turncoats. There's nowhere but a costume party we'd be seen in those shirts now.") Howard liked football and basketball, but not enough to buy a team jersey. He played volleyball in the park occasionally, but what he and his ever-changing group of teammates wore for those sessions was closer to the rags in the free boxes than any coordinated uniform.

What else? He liked to read about the Second World War. He could have joined in on that monologue about the Germans, citing generals, battles, and field strategy. He could have told them Churchill's reactions. Churchill? Hardly. For six-foot-six Howard to pass himself off as the short, portly prime minister would take some disguise. If he could do that, he deserved to keep his parking space.

I took a bite of the taco. The tortilla was crisp, the cheese was sharp, and the salsa was hot enough to make me fling open my mouth to let my tongue cool.

Hitler? I couldn't imagine Howard wanting to spend all evening as Adolf Hitler.

De Gaulle? Ah, de Gaulle. Now there was someone Howard's size. I could see Howard as le Grand Charles.

I put the remains of the taco carefully on my plate, resting it against the side so it wouldn't fall apart. Then I swallowed some Coke. But where would Howard come up with a de Gaulle uniform? There hadn't been anything that resembled that in the costume store today, and besides, I knew he hadn't gotten his costume there. The San Francisco costume store? I'd have to call them. The French consulate in San Francisco?

"Of course," I muttered to my taco. The consulate might know where to get them. There was a phone in the back of the restaurant.

I jammed the rest of the taco into my mouth and got up.

I was halfway across the room before I realized that the remaining piece of taco was too big for my mouth; I could barely close my lips over it, and the attempt to chew sent salsa down my chin, and—I knew even before I looked down—onto my good blouse.

In the bathroom I sponged at the stain on the beige blouse. The water diluted the red salsa to a salmon-colored oval above my left breast. It looked acceptable only to someone who had seen the original red. Maybe if I left my jacket on . . .

The French consulate was even more discouraging. No one answered. Presumably the staff had decided that visiting Parisiens could fend for themselves at night. After all, San Francisco was not Teheran.

And it was ten to eight, too late to go home and change, even if I had had a clean blouse in my closet. I put on my jacket. It covered the stain—if I didn't move my arm. *If I didn't move my arm.* How tame a date was I expecting?

17

Cap Danziger was not in the showroom when I arrived at Trent Cadillac. A man with curly gray hair, who looked more like a business executive than a car salesman, told me he was in the shop.

Thanking him, I followed the path I had taken last night when I'd been headed to see Misco.

The shop was like any other auto repair area—cars lined up in invisible stalls, tubes hanging from the ceiling, man-sized portable diagnostic computers next to several infirm Cadillacs, oil spots and grease. A rear garage door was closed, but through the window a small car lot was visible. Surrounding it was a hurricane fence, ten feet tall, with particularly nasty-looking barbed wire on top. The lot was well lighted. It was not a lot an amateur could break into. Even a professional would have had to devote more time than was practical to broaching the fence.

At the far end of the shop a mechanic was looking under the hood of a silver sedan. Only his white, overalled back and legs were visible. For an instant I wondered if he were Sam Nguyen, but he was too big—and when he stood up—too fair-haired to be the small Vietnamese.

In the near end of the shop a horn tooted. Cap Danziger was leaning in the driver's door of a maroon sedan.

"Want to climb in and see how the other half drives?" he called.

"I think I'm better off not knowing," I said, walking toward him.

He stood up and shut the door. It made a solid clunk. He was wearing a light brown tweed suit with a pale blue shirt. He looked as if he'd sauntered out of *Brideshead Revisited.*

I pulled my jacket closed over the salsa spot.

"You ready for that drink?" he asked, heading toward the street.

"I suppose."

"You don't sound very enthusiastic."

"I am. It's just that I thought for a moment that mechanic was Sam Nguyen and I needed to ask him something." So much for my big resolve not to think about the case on my own time.

"What could he know that he hasn't already been asked? Your friend who deals with cars—"

"Misco."

"Misco, spent hours with him. Sam didn't come in till noon the next day. And Jake Trent had to eat it."

We were on the street now. He paused, then putting a hand on my elbow, headed toward my car. "You didn't answer my question. What more could you want to ask Sam?"

"It wasn't about that. It's just that Ralph Palmerston was furious with him earlier and I need to know what happened."

"Well, you are a lucky lady. I was there."

"You were?" I opened the driver's door, got in, and reached for the lock on the passenger's door.

"Right," he said, climbing in. "Palmerston was waiting for his car to be brought around. I stopped to chat a moment. It's good business to remind the customers who you are. Palmerston spotted Sam as he was headed out the far door. He called. Sam didn't answer; he just kept walking. And Palmerston was fit to be tied. He looked like a head waiter had just poured soup on his lap. I'll tell you, Jill, it took Jake Trent himself a good fifteen minutes to get the old boy calmed down."

"Why didn't Sam Nguyen say anything?"

"Got me. I didn't mention it to him. Sam's got a sharp temper. It's not the type of situation he would want to be reminded of."

I started the engine. "Is he deaf?"

"Could be some. He was in Saigon during the war. There were plenty of explosions and gunfire then."

I pulled into traffic. "The seat belt's behind the door."

"I'll pass."

"I'll feel more comfortable when you have it on. After all, my professional reputation rests on my passengers' safety." When he didn't move I said, "Humor me."

He shrugged, tacitly indicating that he was indeed humoring me in what he found to be ridiculous caution. I felt like Mrs. Kershon trying to protect Billy from germs.

"This isn't a Cadillac," I said. "They say these seats will eject in a bad crash."

"Then they'll mash us into the seat belts."

He had a point.

We rode in silence broken only by his directions. The bar he had in mind was located on The Arlington in Kensington. The Arlington is a road that begins at the Marin traffic circle, where Ralph Palmerston had died. It rises more slowly than Marin Avenue, north into the Berkeley Hills, passing through Berkeley, Kensington, El Cerrito, and Richmond to end near the San Pablo Reservoir. For me, it was even more questionable than Marin Avenue. That, I knew I'd never climb, but with The Arlington, there was a possibility. And with Cap Danziger in the car, I didn't want to admit that my Volkswagen couldn't make a hill that he thought nothing of. It was tantamount to showing him my salsa stain.

So I drove in silence, listening to the engine, judging

how long to let it labor before shifting down, wondering why it was that we were in my car when Cap Danziger worked at a place whose lowliest model was worth thousands more, and wondering what it was about this man that made me hesitate to ask, and that made me feel I had to prove myself to him, had to prove my car was as good as his.

But if Cap Danziger noticed my underlying competitiveness, he didn't acknowledge it. Half a mile before the block-long shopping area of Kensington, I downshifted to first gear. He didn't comment.

"Not exactly a Cadillac," I admitted.

"I'll take your word. I'm almost totally innocent of mechanical knowledge. An engine is an engine as long as it runs." He motioned me to a parking spot.

Gratefully I pulled in and turned off the ignition, got out, and followed him down an alleyway to a plain wooden door that led into a small, square, oak-paneled room. In one corner a woman played a viola. We settled at a table at the far side of the room.

After we ordered, I said, "I thought that someone who sold cars would have to know everything there was about engines. Don't your customers ask?"

He laughed. "I'm relieved to hear you say that. That's exactly what I assumed when I asked about the job. I have a cousin who gave me a crash course—no pun intended—on carburetors, power steering, and RPMs so I could sound automobile-literate when I was interviewed for the position. But I never needed it. Marv Belkowski—he owned the dealership before Jake Trent; everyone there except Sam is new within the last couple of years—didn't waste time on fan belts or EPA ratios. He knew that Cadillac buyers aren't going to ask about that. You see, Jill," he said, resting his fingers on my arm, "anyone who buys a Cadillac isn't doing it for the engine; they've got their own reasons."

"Such as?"

"Fulfillment of a dream; indication that they've made it. Snob appeal. A Cadillac's not just a good car, it's a Cadillac. It's not like deciding between a Nissan and a Toyota."

"So what do you sell your customers on, then?"

He smiled again. "I grace them with my patrician upbringing. I speak to them in my refined accent. I drop a few key words about performance, just for form's sake—they never ask for specifics. If they did, I'd take them to Sam Nguyen. But they don't. I am like the very correct British gentleman's gentleman. Customers are not about to expose their ignorance in front of me. It's all part of the snob appeal."

"But surely some—"

"Not in the five years I've been there. Even the drug dealers—I suppose I should say gentlemen I assume to be drug dealers—don't ask what's under the hood."

Our drinks arrived. I sipped my Cinzano, and asked, "What do your reputed drug dealers care about?"

He stared down into his glass, as if giving my offhand question serious thought. In the candlelight his sandy hair glistened. There were lines across his forehead and by the sides of his mouth, lines I hadn't noticed in the sunlight, but rather than making him appear older, they seemed to accentuate the consideration he was showing my question. "Some drug dealers do ask about pickup. Having a fast engine can increase their margin of profit, I understand."

"And their longevity."

"Others, of course, focus on the exterior, the paint. Opera windows were big a few years ago. Landau roofs are still drawing cards. And for those with more money, the draw is Sam Nguyen."

"Sam Nguyen! Is he involved in drugs?"

"No, no. Anything but. Sam is more firmly opposed to drugs than the strictest conservatives. He blames the drug trade for the downfall of his country. No, Sam's attraction is that he is simply the best automotive modifier around. He can make any change in a car, no matter how absurd it sounds. He prides himself on never being stymied."

"I've heard high praise of Sam Nguyen myself."

"Oh, he's the best. No question. Jake Trent keeps close tabs on his mechanics. With our customers, if anything's out of place there's hell to pay. But Sam—well, Sam doesn't consider himself in the same class as the other mechanics. He's an artisan. He doesn't deal with the mechanics at all, except when he needs to have one of them lift a fender or hold a cable out of the way. He struts in in the morning like he owns the service bay. When the union guys break for coffee, Sam keeps on working. At noon, the union guys stop for lunch; Sam works. But then, at one on the dot, he puts down his tools and drives to the Bien Hoa Vietnamese Restaurant in Oakland. I went there with him once." He smiled as if to say that he had passed Nguyen's strict muster. "At the restaurant they treat him like a king. When he arrives, a masseuse is at the door. She gives him twenty minutes. And when she's done, his lunch is waiting, all five courses. The waiters hover, the owner grovels. Sam compliments them. The other Vietnamese smile. And then Sam's car is brought around and he leaves. By the time he gets back to the shop it's two-thirty or quarter to three."

"And your boss doesn't mind?"

"Sam could come back at six and it would be okay with Jake Trent. Trent's no dummy. He's pleased to have Sam as long as Sam will stay."

I finished my drink.

Cap signaled the waiter, with the same aplomb that I imagined of Sam Nguyen.

"So you sell the cars to drug dealers for their opera windows and Sam Nguyen. For everyone else it's just snob appeal?"

The viola stopped. It had been so soft that it was a

moment before the twelve or so of us patrons applauded. Cap cocked his head slightly, as if he were pondering a quizzical situation. "I'm afraid you credit the drug dealers too highly, Jill. They're as much into snob appeal as the next guy. They love being the men with the cash; it flatters them to have someone with a cultured accent pulling out the ashtrays and opening the hoods for them." He sighed. "Snob appeal is one of the few constants in life—it cuts through all social strata. Even in 'Society,' where I am accepted because of my very proper forebears, there's as much clawing to get to the very top. You're judged by who you know, how much money you have, and what family you are connected to. Lucky for me." He laughed. "Because I am a New England Danziger I can be invited places no ordinary car salesman would be permitted."

"Sounds like the Danziger breeding is to your friends what opera windows are to the dealers."

"Exactly. Only in Society the rules are stricter. If they knew I laughed at them like this . . ."

"Or was drinking with a common cop?"

"Once would be okay. I could even bring you, in all your 'commonness' "—he favored me with a grin—"to a charity ball. But if they found out that I had abused the code . . . if I did it again . . . Well, twice is just not acceptable."

I had promised myself I wouldn't think about the case tonight. But I couldn't resist asking. "I'm dealing with a woman—very attractive, an actress, who met her husband at one of these Society affairs. As far as I know she had no family connections. How do you think she managed to be accepted?"

The waitress leaned over the table, picking up the ashtray and replacing it with a fresh one, even though the original was unused. She glanced at our glasses then moved on.

"One of the advantages of having social connections,

other than in business—I do sell a few cars to men I've met at those affairs. Jake Trent isn't above appreciating their patronage. He gets to be a snob to the other Cadillac dealers. But the amusing advantage is having its odd customs to talk about. It keeps people from finding me too dull."

"So how did this woman make her way into the magic circle?"

"Well, she might have met her man on her first try before anyone discovered she was not sterling but silver plate. Or as an actress, well, actresses are in a class by themselves. But most likely, if she wasn't offensive, was decorative, and did and said the right things and—and this is important—sincerely believed in the overriding importance of Society, she could hang on for a while as a not-quite-respectable fringe member. But it would be easier if her family had a name, and money." He lifted his glass and took a swallow. "But enough chatter about me and my peculiar connections. What about you? Do you have a line on your murderer yet? It is a murder, I assume, since you're a Homicide officer."

"Murder cases require a lot of legwork before any lines are clear."

"Don't you get hunches? Don't you come to sense who's being honest with you and who's trying to put you on?"

I laughed. "No one is honest with the police. Not totally. Even people who are only remotely connected to the case are uneasy in the presence of a cop. They consider their answers. They fidget. They say too little or too much. They look guilty as hell. As a rule, the killer looks no more suspect than the rest."

He finished his drink and leaned back in his chair. "So how do you decide who to concentrate on? In the case you're working on now, for instance, you must have a few suspects. How do you narrow down the field?"

"Actually, I don't in this case. The problem is not too many suspects but too few."

The waiter arrived with our drinks.

Cap fingered his glass. His hands were long, his fingers slender but surprisingly firm, as if they belonged to a sculptor. But unlike a sculptor's hands, which would have shown the cuts and bruises of misaimed hits, Cap's hands were smooth. They suited his patrician accent. They were hands his customers would approve of. They were hands that seemed capable of caressing and controlling.

Aware that I was staring, I moved my gaze to the candle. Before I realized it, I had yawned.

Cap laughed. "I told you I had to keep talking about my Society connections or you'd find me dull."

"It's certainly not you," I said quickly. "This is the most pleasant evening I've had in a while. It's just that I was up till three this morning"—I couldn't resist adding —"at the morgue."

"You're going to tell me then you had to set your alarm for six?"

"We have to be up before our prey."

"What time is that?" He took a swallow of his drink, making an effort to finish it.

"Detectives' Morning Meeting is at quarter to eight."

"That's not too uncivilized."

"It wouldn't be," I said, picking up my own glass, "if it weren't for the parking."

Perhaps it was the lack of food—I had eaten only the taco on my taco special plate this evening. Perhaps it was my embarrassment at yawning or maybe just the effect of Cap Danziger himself, but I felt distinctly uneasy, and in that unease I talked about the department's parking problems. I talked about them as we left the bar, as we walked to the car, and by the time I was driving down the hill, I was telling Cap Danziger about my bet with Howard and my failure to discover his costume. Howard's costume seemed to hold special interest for him, as if he were entering the game.

"My best guess is he'll come as de Gaulle."

"French restaurants," he said.

"What about them?"

"Some have pretty fancy waiters. I wouldn't put it past the more ornate ones to have a Grand Charles maitre d'."

"Really?"

"Ludicrous as it sounds."

I sighed. "Halloween's tomorrow. It would take me plenty longer than that to call every French restaurant in the Bay Area." I slowed down.

"I think I can help."

"You can?"

"A friend of mine is a maitre d'. I can give him a call. He'd know where any de Gaulle is working."

"That's great."

"Why don't we stop at your place. I can call him now. This is a good time for him, the early rush will be over, the after-theater crowd won't be in yet. Then I can walk home."

"It's raining."

"Just a drizzle. I have a raincoat."

I tried to remember what shape I had left my apartment in. At the best of times I was not a good housekeeper. My cleaning standards matched my eating habits. Neither provided examples I would want to be seen by my mother, or by Cap Danziger. Only my lack of possessions saved the place from being a real shambles.

I pulled up in front of the Kepple house. As I reached for the car door, I started to warn him that he wasn't headed to a place he'd be likely to see in *Architectural Digest*. But he would find that out soon enough.

I led him around the side of the Kepple house to my jalousied porch apartment. In summer the jalousies on three sides allowed the cool breeze to flow through. Sleeping there was like camping out. In winter it was definitely like camping. The aluminum walls beneath the windows and the aluminum siding that covered the rear wall of the house were icy. I opened the door and flicked on the light. To my right my sleeping bag lay in a heap where I'd tossed it. The green indoor-outdoor carpet had been vacuumed a week or so ago and wasn't in too bad shape. Even the puddles under the jalousies had shrunk during the day and could be cleared in one step. If it hadn't been for the white wicker table, the place would have been passable.

All that was visible of the table top was a circle in front of the chair where I'd sat to drink coffee and eat croissants last Sunday while I had read—what? An issue from the two-foot-high pile of Sunday *New York Times* on the table, or daily *Chronicle*s stacked next to them, or one of the *New Yorker*s that went back to July? Or perhaps I had glanced at a NOW newsletter, or one from Friends of the Sea Otter. Or maybe I'd checked the UC Theater listings, or a catalog from Cal Extension or L. L. Bean, or Early Winters, Pepperidge Farms, Community Kitchens, J. Crew, Eddie Bauer, Sporting Dog, or any of the twenty or so others strewn there. The table resembled nothing so much as a recycling bin. I was just relieved that the coffee cup had made it to the kitchen.

There was nothing to do but ignore the mess. "The phone is next to the chaise lounge," I said, indicating the far end of the room. The chaise lounge, another item more suitable to a campsite or at least the backyard, was plastic, but in deference to winter I had bought a flowered cushion to block out the drafts from the jalousies. When the lounge was empty, the cushion puffed up like an infected finger.

Cap didn't comment on the room. He gave no indication of noticing anything untoward. Was that, I wondered, what was meant by "good breeding"?

He picked up the phone and dialed. Sitting on the lounge he waited, then asked for Ivan Henry.

I started to take my jacket off, then remembered the salsa spot.

"Cap Danziger," he said, and then repeated my phone number. Replacing the receiver, he looked up at me. "Ivan's on break. They'll have him call as soon as he gets back. That shouldn't be long. I've been there; they don't give their employees a minute more off than the union requires."

"You might as well make yourself comfortable, then. Can I get you something? I've taken to having hot buttered rum on cold evenings."

"Sounds good," he said.

I could tell from experience with other guests that he was bemused at just how to go about getting comfortable. The only way to approach it was to crawl into the chaise lounge, lean against the back, and pull your feet up. Invariably that was an awkward thing for a guest to do. They felt ungracious leaving me to clear off a wicker chair.

But Cap Danziger adjusted himself further onto the lounge, resting his elbows on the chair arms. In his light brown suit, against the paisley cushions and the jalousies, he looked as if he'd just wandered in from safari.

When I returned with the drinks, I handed him his mug. "Take it by the handle; it's hot."

He stared down at the mug before taking hold.

"My ex-husband got the crystal," I said by way of explanation. "He was going to be a college professor. We agreed professors are more likely to need crystal than cops."

He glanced around the room again, pursed his lips as if trying to restrain himself, and then said, "What did *you* get?"

I laughed. He wasn't the first to ask that. Both Howard and Pereira had surveyed this same bare room and been brought to the same inquiry.

"Half the *National Geographic*s, for one thing. But mainly the car."

Now he laughed. "At least you didn't have much to fight over."

I said nothing.

"It would have been nice if you'd gotten the bed," he added.

"There was no bed. We slept on the floor."

"You mean he got the floor?"

"Just about."

He shifted toward the head of the lounge in unspoken invitation for me to join him on it. I sat.

"It's a nice room," he said, "like a basement recreation room where all the games are kept, where you can do whatever you want."

I smiled. He was the first one who had understood that.

Still, I avoided his eyes, not sure whether I wanted to let myself fall under their mesmerizing gaze. I hadn't planned to invite him in. Other than Howard, I hadn't invited a man here at all. I'd wanted to keep control. But I hadn't met a man as attractive before.

He drew me toward him with the slightest of touches, took the glass from my hand. His lips were teasingly soft, more distant than close, beckoning me.

The phone rang.

"Damn," he said, releasing me.

I shook myself back to reality and reached for the phone. Involuntarily I glanced at my watch. It was nearly eleven, too late for any of my friends to call me on a work night.

"Hello?"

"Detective Smith?" The voice—a woman's—was shaky.

"Yes?"

"Lois Palmerston. I . . . I called . . . before. No answer."

"Are you all right?" She sounded as if she was falling apart.

"Yes . . . No . . . Look, I need . . . I don't know. Can you come here?"

"Now, Lois?"

"Yes. Please, now."

I hesitated momentarily, avoiding Cap's gaze. "Okay. Give me a few minutes. You know how long it takes me to get my car up the hill."

There was a small sound on the phone line—an inadvertent whine of fear. "Yes, but you will come, won't you?"

"I'm coming now. I'll be right there." I put down the receiver.

Turning to Cap, I gave his hand a squeeze. "I'm sorry, really. It's business and I have to go now. The drawbacks of being a cop."

He kept hold of my hand. "Another time. Soon. After all, I need to call you when I find out about de Gaulle."

Grabbing my purse, I led him out the door and to the car. I dropped him on Shattuck and headed toward the hills.

The Lois Palmerston I had talked to on the phone bore no resemblance to the cool, beautiful woman I had seen last night. What had happened to make her fall apart so quickly?

18

The Palmerston house was just as dark and empty-looking as it had been at seven when I had talked with Billy Kershon. I turned off the ignition and watched for movement inside, but there was none. Had Lois Palmerston been so distraught that she'd forgotten where she was when she called me?

The light at the gate was off, but I had been here often enough to find the bell. I rang. The rain ran along my hair, into my collar, down the back of my jacket. I could, I thought, have been curled up on the chaise lounge with the most attractive man I'd met in years; instead I was standing in the rain outside the house of a woman who might not be home. Or worse, a woman who had been here twenty-five minutes ago and now was gone, or who was unable to get to the door.

But the door opened a crack, and the gate buzzer sounded, and I pulled the gate open.

"Have you been sitting with the light out all evening long?" I asked as I walked in the front door.

In the dark, she seemed to be nodding.

I felt for the light and turned it on.

When I had seen her this morning, Lois Palmerston had looked unstrung, but now she was a wreck. The combs had fallen out and her hair hung in stiff, reddish-blond clumps, some clumps swaying out to the side from where the combs had trained them, others hanging limp along her neck. There was a streak of ash across her cheek, and ground-in ash on her silk pants. She'd dribbled coffee on her blouse. She looked more like a chronic alcoholic than the woman I had seen last night.

She pressed her thumb against her cheek to steady her hand as she moved a cigarette to her mouth. The house was thick with smoke. I took her arm and propelled her into the living room, then felt in the likely spot for the light switch and turned on the lights. She started.

Sitting her down on the sofa, I said, "Now what is the matter? Tell me."

She drew in long on the cigarette. "They're . . . they're going to get me."

"Who?"

"Just like they did to Ralph. It'll be easier with me. They'll just come."

"Who? Who is going to get you?"

She looked over at me as if seeing me for the first time. "I can't tell you."

"You *can* tell me," I said in a calm voice.

"No. They'd find out."

"I'm a police officer. I can protect you."

"No one can help me. They're outside."

"Now?"

"Maybe. I don't know. Before. Before I called you. I heard them then."

"Were they trying to break into the garage?"

"No, not the garage. I would have heard the door go up."

"Where, then? Where were they coming in?"

"The front window."

I looked at the picture window, the lower half covered with wooden shutters. It didn't open. But the one near it on the side of the house did. "I'm going to look around outside. You just stay here."

"No. Don't go."

"I'll only be right outside. You can see me through the windows."

She stared blankly at me. I took her by the hand and walked her to a spot where she could see out both windows. I considered asking her for a flashlight, but even that request seemed more than she could handle. Instead I ran to my car and extricated the one in the glove compartment.

Through the rain I flashed the light along the window frame. There were no marks. But since this window didn't open, there was no reason there would be. And in the state Lois Palmerston was in, it was questionable whether any menace had existed except in her own imagination. In front of the window were three or four small bushes that had grown together, forming a low hedge that reached just to the window. Three feet of grass separated the street and the hedge. I flashed the light on the bushes but they looked intact. Then I let the light fall to the grass.

There were footprints on the grass. The ground was soft from the rain. The prints must have been fairly clear when they were made, but by now any identifying information had been washed away. From their general shape, particularly the squared-off heel, they looked like they had been made by running shoes.

I followed the footprints to the corner of the front window. Again, I checked the window itself, but there were definitely no marks on the frame.

Behind the wooden shutters Lois Palmerston stared at me, her hazel eyes wide in terror. They looked as if they'd drawn the life from the rest of her pallid face. I forced myself to smile at her and point to the side window. Then I aimed the flashlight down. The prints suggested the running-shoed figure had stepped back from the front window, perhaps when he realized it didn't open, and moved around to the one at the side. The prints led right up beneath it.

Because of the steep slope of the lot, the side window was a foot farther off the ground than the front one, so that entering here would not be a question of just stepping inside, as one might have from an open front window, but of hoisting up and climbing in. The attempt would have left visible marks on the window frame. I let the light fall on the bush beneath the window. Several small branches were broken. I moved the light up to the frame, ran it along the edges, up one side and down the other, and along the bottom twice. But there were no signs of attempted entry. There were no marks at all.

I focused the light on the ground. The drop to the backyard was steep. The next window back was eight feet off the ground. If anyone were going to break in, it would be through the side window. And unless Lois had turned it off, the house was protected by a burglar alarm system.

Lois was staring down at me. I smiled again and shook my head. Then I aimed the light down. The footprints went no farther. They looked as if they had backed up the way they'd come. But the rain was getting heavier and it was no longer possible to discern which were the toe-heavy forward steps and which the more even backings away.

Motioning to Lois, I moved back to the sidewalk. Without any expectations, I tried the garage door. It didn't move. By the time I got back inside, the rain had soaked into my jacket again.

Lois was standing at the door shivering. Now, in my wet jacket, I realized how cold it was in this house.

"Haven't you put the heat on?" I asked.

"I never turn it on. Ralph always did that."

There were no floor heaters, as many California houses have. This one would have the more expensive central heating. I looked for the thermostat and turned it up to seventy-two. Then I took her by the arm and sat her down on a sofa. I felt as if I were shifting a mannequin.

"You were right," I said. "There was someone out

there tonight. But there are no marks on the windows. So either they decided not to break in or they never intended to. Now, Mrs. Palmerston, who would have reason to be out there under your windows?"

"I don't know."

"You said 'they.' Who are 'they'?"

"I don't know."

"You must have some idea, some suspicion."

"No. I don't know. I don't know." Her voice had the same pale, ethereal quality as her face. I couldn't decide if she really didn't know, or if she just couldn't summon the energy to put her suspicions into words. She stabbed out her cigarette in the ashtray. A quick glance showed me that every ashtray in the room was overflowing. She'd been chain-smoking since I had left her last night. If she was going to be at all lucid, she needed food.

"We're going to the kitchen," I said. "I'll fix you something to eat."

"I can't eat."

"Of course you can." Taking her by the arm, I half pulled her up.

The kitchen was a big remodeled room with portico windows. The center island held a stove, a chopping block, and a counter with two stools. Lois was in no condition to balance on a stool. I left her leaning against the counter.

Thankful that Inspector Doyle couldn't see this, I scrambled eggs, toasted bread, and found some cocoa in a cabinet. I made enough for two.

"Eat," I said before she could protest. "You haven't eaten in thirty-six hours; you can eat. Now go ahead."

She ate, hesitantly at first, then mechanically. I toasted more bread and she ate that.

When she was done, I said, "Now I want you to tell me what is going on."

"I'm afraid."

"Yes?"

"The people who killed my husband, they're going to kill me."

"Who are they?"

"I don't know."

"Why would they want to kill you?"

She shook her head.

"You must have some idea."

"No. I told you, I don't. Stop pushing me."

I took a breath. "Mrs. Palmerston, you called me at home when I had company. I left my house, and my guest, to come up here because you asked. Now the least you can do is to make an effort to discover what you are afraid of."

She lit a cigarette and said, as if she were talking to an idiot, "There was someone outside."

"True. But you don't suspect it was a prowler or a burglar. You didn't call for a beat officer. You called for a Homicide detective. You figured the person outside was someone connected with your husband's murder. Now what makes you think that?"

She just shrugged and smoked.

"Mrs. Palmerston, you say you're afraid of your husband's killer, but you do everything in your power to keep me from finding that person. You wouldn't talk to me earlier. You wouldn't let me inside. Then you filed a harassment complaint. After all that, you call me and tell me you're afraid. Now what is it you expect me to do about that?"

"I expect you to protect me," she said in a surprisingly steady voice. "I'm a taxpayer. We pay a lot of taxes to the city. I expect protection."

I pressed my fist into the chopping board. "The police department is not a guard agency. We do investigations. If you want a twenty-four-hour guard, get a Doberman." Before she could respond, I said, "Now I'm going to go through the house to make sure no one did get in."

I hurried out of the kitchen, through the dining room,

and up the stairs before she could follow me. There was no one else in the house; I was sure of that. But I was also sure that Lois Palmerston was no more likely to allow me to search the house now than she had been earlier today. I could see in her the woman who had lived off the Munsons for years and then not deigned to invite them to her wedding. If lack of reciprocity were cash, Lois wouldn't have needed Ralph Palmerston's money.

The second floor consisted of three rooms and two baths. For form's sake I checked the master bedroom and the large bathroom. Then crossing the hall, I listened, but there was no sound of Lois approaching. Either she knew I wouldn't find anything useful up here, or she *believed* that I was looking for an assailant and she wanted to keep out of the line of fire. Or exhaustion had caught up with her and she was too tired to bother.

Of the two small rooms, one was a guest room. I checked the dresser drawers and closet but there was nothing but spare blankets there. Making my way through the adjoining bathroom, I came to what looked like an office. It was done in mahogany—heavy desk, bookshelves, green leather swivel chair. It looked like an office where John Farrell, the lawyer, would have felt at home.

I listened again, but still there was no sound of Lois approaching. It would take time to search through all the desk drawers and the closet for Ott's reports, more time than could be explained by looking for an intruder.

I started with the center desk drawer. I pulled it open. On top, was a brown $8\frac{1}{2} \times 11$ envelope. Sliding the papers out, I found Ott's reports.

I turned to the last page of the bottom report. I was in luck. In caps, it was headed SUMMARY:

Persuant to your instructions of September and subsequent, I have made inquiries about the five persons you indicated, their compelling interests and what is vital to the sustenance of said interests:

Adam Thede—Sunny Sides Up health food breakfast restaurant. Suppliers of non-organic vegetables: J & R Farms (pesticide use); Oliver Hernandez Farms (herbicide use). Always Fresh Bakery (wheat procured from G.P. Fulmot of Topeka, Kansas, which uses herbicides and pesticides and sells to commercial bakeries). ["9/26" was handwritten in pencil.]

Carol Grogan—1397 Ordway, Berkeley dwelling. Second mortgage in arrears since June of this year. Holder Peter Hargis. Mr. Hargis is willing to sell for a significant profit. ["10/12" was handwritten in pencil.]

Nina Munson—handcrafted jackets sold at Amber Crescent (owner Ruth Katz), Handmade Wraps (owner Estelle Usher), the Normandy (owner Thomas Juriss), and One of a Kind (owners Grace and Robert Simmons.) ["10/25" was in pencil.]

Jeffrey Munson—Munsonalysis. Accepted contract from Von Slocum Mining five years ago. Von Slocum is a major supplier of small mining equipment to South Africa.

As we agreed re: your subject at Trent Cadillac, the conclusion is too obvious to require my services.

This report, following the three preliminary reports, concludes our contract regarding those persons known as Shareholders Five. It has been a pleasure being of service to you.

The report was signed by Herman Ott.

I sat staring at it. Nina and Jeffrey Munson, and—Jesus Christ!—Sam Nguyen.

Or could he possibly have meant—I swallowed—Cap Danziger? I didn't even want to consider that and its implications. I started riffling through the pages of the full report. Maybe Ott had been less cryptic there. Damn Herman Ott and his professional ethics. Any other pri-

vate eye would have taken Palmerston's money for the
fifth Shareholder and considered it a gift. I skimmed the
pages. I had to know who this fifth member of the group
was. Was it possible that the man who had been kissing
me on my chaise lounge was involved in Ralph Palmerston's murder?

Trips to Salinas, Visalia, Delano motels, charges for
meals, phone calls, car rentals; Herman Ott was thorough.

"What do you think you're doing?" Lois stood at the
door, one hand on her hip, the other holding a cigarette.
In my rush to find out what Ott had done, to find out
about Cap Danziger, I had completely forgotten Lois
Palmerston.

"This is a report from the detective your husband
hired," I said, standing up. "You knew about this, didn't
you?"

"You don't have any right to go through his desk. I
didn't say you could do that."

"The report wasn't hidden. It was in the first place
anyone would look. You knew it was here. There's no
need to deny it. You knew what was in it. And you knew
why your husband was getting this information. Now
why was that?"

"I want you to put that back where you found it and
leave my house."

"You called and begged me to come here."

"That's what you say."

I stared. I hadn't expected this level of duplicity. I took
a breath. Inspector Doyle's face flashed before me. I
didn't want to think how he would react to a second
complaint in two days. The woman was a pro. She'd
probably throw in my crack about the Doberman, too.
But I wasn't about to leave. "Mrs. Palmerston, the people
mentioned in this report are your friends. Why was your
husband checking up on them? What is it that connects
the Munsons and Carol Grogan?"

"I told you to leave."

"I'll go when you answer my questions."

She stared at me. I returned her gaze. It was a moment before she looked down and took a drag of her cigarette.

"All right," she said. "I'm going to tell you what I told Ralph about those people and then I expect you to leave. Is that a promise?"

"We don't make promises in Homicide investigations."

She looked like she was going to argue and then suddenly found the effort too great. "Come downstairs," she said. "I'm tired."

I followed her to the living room and sat next to her on one of the sofas. She stubbed out her cigarette and immediately lit another.

"I needed money. I borrowed it from my friends, from the people mentioned in the detective's report. I never told Ralph until he heard from the doctor, that he was going blind."

I said nothing, waiting.

"It was a very emotional time for both Ralph and me. I shouldn't have told him; I wasn't in control. But we were afraid; we thought at first that his eye problem came from a brain tumor. You don't last long when you have one of those. We thought he was going to die."

Still I waited.

"Like I said, it was a very emotional time. All of a sudden, he wanted me to tell him everything. Up till then he hadn't wanted to know anything about me before I met him, I mean anything really personal. Now he wanted everything. He wanted to know what my childhood was like, what courses I'd taken in college, how I'd lived afterward. He wanted to hear about every man I'd dated, every one I'd slept with, who I'd borrowed money from. Ralph said he wanted to make restitution before he died. He wanted to leave the world with a clean slate. So I told him. I'd taken money from friends."

"How much had you borrowed?"

"Oh, I don't know—"

"Mrs. Palmerston, your husband asked you this question. He wanted to know how much. You told him. You know. Now how much?"

"Five thousand dollars."

"Each?"

"Yes."

I restrained a whistle. Lois Palmerston certainly could get the most out of people. To Carol Grogan and Nina and Jeffrey Munson, five thousand dollars would have been a great deal of money. I asked, "When was that?"

"Five years ago."

"Why? For what?"

She swallowed. "Officer Smith," she said in a low, very controlled voice. "I've answered your questions. I'm distraught. My husband was killed yesterday." She looked at her watch. "Two days ago now. It's after midnight. I haven't slept in God knows when. If you don't leave right now, I am going to call my lawyer at home."

"Just one more question. Who was the person at Trent Cadillac?" I held my breath.

"No. That's all."

There was an icy desperation to her words. I knew I'd get nothing else out of her, except another complaint. I stood up.

"Put the detective's report down," she said.

I did, and left.

19

The thought of going home passed through my mind only briefly. If I was going to be awake and furious, I might as well do it at the station dictating my report. Maybe Lois Palmerston would file another complaint anyway. I'd gone out of my way to accommodate her. I should have known better. Nine to five, they'd told us in patrol officer training; don't take your work home with you. You only end up screwing yourself. And don't give extra services, I could have added, and then expect to get something in return for them, particularly from someone with a record of using people like Lois Palmerston's. Four years on the force; I should have known better.

I crossed University at King Way, running the red light after the two cars ahead of me. Cars on University hit their horns. I blew mine back.

What I really wished was that I had Cap Danziger's home address, that I could go there and yank him out of his patrician bed, and force the truth out of him.

I pulled up by the station. There was a spot in front. I wasn't even pleased. Goddamnit, I wished Howard was here to talk to. I could go by his house. For his house this wasn't too late.

But I paused only momentarily. I wasn't going to discuss *this* with Howard. Or with Pereira. After a year of complaints about my ex-husband, I wasn't about to admit to my friends that the first man I was attracted to was probably up to his ears in my murder case.

I headed inside, dumped my purse on my desk, and pulled the one new message from my IN box. It was in Howard's scrawl: *Lois P. clear with SFPD Vice.*

So Lois hadn't been involved in prostitution in San Francisco, or at least she'd never been picked up or even suspected. Another time I would have been disappointed at that dead end. Now, I was still too angry. I took my notes and walked to the dictation booths.

"Lois Palmerston, widow of the deceased," I began, "called me at home at ten-thirty. She sounded shaky— see earlier report on her condition—and asked me several times to come to her house." I realized I had deleted any mention of Cap Danziger being at my house when the call came.

I went on describing the footprints outside Lois's windows. Stopping, I wondered who had made those prints. In running shoes, it could have been a man or a woman. It could have been ninety percent of the Berkeley population. Was it one of the Shareholders Five? Why would they be looking in Lois's window, particularly if the house was dark? To see if they could break in and get Ott's report? That made sense. But that also meant they knew of the existence of the report. Had Ralph told them? I felt sure that Ott, oddly professional Herman Ott, would never have revealed his assignment to the subjects of it. But if one of the five wanted to get that report, then the only logical reason was so that I wouldn't find it and connect them to Ralph Palmerston's murder.

I was beginning to feel better.

I described Lois Palmerston's appearance, forwent any mention of the eggs and cocoa, and detailed my search of the premises and discovery of Ott's report. Its contents I dictated as specifically as I could recall:

Adam Thede, his health food restaurant, and his tainted suppliers.

Carol Grogan, her house, and the overdue second mortgage.

Jeffrey Munson, Munsonalysis, and his contract with the South African supplier.

Nina Munson, her handmade jackets, and three of the four stores I could recall.

And "our friend at Trent Cadillac," for whom Herman Ott had found no professional expertise necessary.

Controlling my resurgence of anger, I dictated Lois's explanation of the list: her story that she had borrowed five thousand dollars from each of her friends, and that Ralph Palmerston had wanted to make restitution before he lost his sight. Did I believe that story? At a time like that, talking about childhood was understandable. Lovers —I could see that. But discussing outstanding personal debts was an odd inclusion. And despite whatever he might have told Herman Ott, Ralph Palmerston hadn't done anything good for Adam Thede. It was possible that his information had come too late, as Thede suggested. What about Carol Grogan? Palmerston hadn't paid the back payments on her second mortgage. Surely, he was the one who bought it from Peter Hargis. He could have canceled the entire mortgage. But if he had done that, Carol Grogan wouldn't have called Lois to ask for a loan —if that indeed was the reason she had contacted Lois.

Nina? It wouldn't be difficult to see if those stores were carrying her jackets.

Jeffrey? What good would it do him to know a contract he'd signed five years ago was with a South African supplier? For someone with Jeffrey's radical pretensions, dealing with a South African–connected firm would be devastating. In Berkeley, that type of publicity could cripple Munsonalysis. But Jeffrey still seemed to be in business. Unlike Adam Thede, nothing bad had happened to him.

But what was so obvious about Cap Danziger's interests? In what way would Ralph have helped him? Cap was handsome and charming, and had good connections. All he lacked was money. If Ralph Palmerston had done something good for Cap—given him money—Cap wouldn't have been working late, night after night. If he had money, he would certainly have a car; we wouldn't have driven to the bar in my car last night. So it wasn't *good* that Ralph Palmerston had in mind for Cap. Did he instead plan to get him fired from Trent? As a punishment that wasn't in the same league as losing the restaurant of your dreams, where you had the only opportunity to be creative in the world of vegetarian breakfasts. Losing one job selling cars merely meant that Cap Danziger would move to another. Car salesmen changed jobs all the time.

I sat back, idly listening to the guy in the next booth describing an assault on Telegraph. David Thomas, seller of feather ornaments, had attacked bodily one Timothy Arndt, seller of tie-dyed T-shirts on the next blanket, after Arndt's springer spaniel had become too familiar with Thomas's wares. Both principals were under arrest. The springer spaniel, presumably, was home with the T-shirts (and maybe a few contraband feathers).

I walked to the machine and got a cup of coffee. At two-thirty in the morning it tasted awful.

What if "our friend at Trent Cadillac" was not Cap Danziger but Sam Nguyen? (It had to be one of the two; they were the only Trent employees at the dealership five years ago.) I hesitated to even consider the possibility for fear I would be misled by my own desires. But if Clayton Jackson's conclusion about Lois Palmerston—that she was dealing cocaine—was correct, then it would make sense that her connection was not Cap Danziger but Sam Nguyen. Sam Nguyen might be known as being adamantly opposed to drugs, but dealers hardly advertised their trade. Sam Nguyen may just have worked out a good cover. He could still have connections in the Far

East. And if he aimed to open his own garage, what easier way to get money?

But how would Lois have come in contact with him? Could she have met him sometime when Ralph picked up his car? No, she had got the money from the Shareholders Five five years ago, before she knew Palmerston. But Jeffrey had worked as a mechanic when he first arrived in Berkeley. He would have known Sam Nguyen. If Sam Nguyen were the drug connection, that would mean that instead of being one of the five Shareholders "loaning" money to Lois, he had been the recipient. It would mean that the fifth Shareholder was not Sam (or Cap) but Lois.

I gathered up my notes. Lois Palmerston had come out here five years ago in the summer. Almost immediately she persuaded four or five people to "loan" her five thousand dollars. Why, but for a highly profitable drug deal, would a woman like Carol Grogan, divorced, with two young children and a house payment she could barely manage, be willing to loan a strange woman five thousand dollars? How did she even raise that money?

To Ralph Palmerston, making money off the weaknesses of others would hardly seem "courteous." Lois had lied to him, told him the money was a loan. Had Ralph been suspicious of her story, just as I was? Had he hired Herman Ott to find out what was really going on? That sounded like something important enough for a man to get settled before he went blind. Had he found that Sam Nguyen had lured Lois and the other four into the drug world? Or had he assumed all five of them (Sam and the four Shareholders) had corrupted the wife he cared for? Had he then instructed Herman Ott to begin with the part of the investigation that I had discovered in his report?

One thing was clear. There was no evidence Ralph Palmerston had done anyone a good turn, and plenty of reason to assume he had planned to hurt them.

It was a moment before I realized the irony of Ralph

Palmerston's retribution. Five years ago Carol Grogan had taken a second mortgage on her house. That had to be where she got the money to give Lois. And it was that house that Ralph had been threatening when he bought the second mortgage.

And Nina Munson. I recalled her saying that five years ago she had made the pivotal sacrifice of selling her mother's antique necklace. Had she used the proceeds for Lois or, as she implied, to finance designing and making her jackets? It was her designing that Ralph had zeroed in on.

Adam Thede? The connection was not so clear. But he had told me Sunny Sides Up had been in business six months, and he'd waited for almost five years to open it. It sounded like five years ago he had diverted enough money to keep his dream in abeyance. It also sounded like Ralph Palmerston hadn't waited long before spreading the news of Thede's tainted suppliers.

Coming back to Sam Nguyen, five years ago would have been a reasonable time for him to have immigrated to the United States. Was it with the Immigration Service that Ralph Palmerston had planned to deal his retribution to Sam Nguyen? The Immigration Service takes a dim view of drug dealing.

I plunked my pad and pencil on my desk. My theory was good, but it was just a theory. There was nothing substantial linking Lois Palmerston or Sam Nguyen to cocaine, or any other drugs, for that matter. I needed some evidence, or at least a good lead.

There was one person who would know who was dealing drugs in Berkeley, and if there had been a twenty-five-thousand dollar deal five years ago. That was Leon Evans.

Without thinking, I glanced at Howard's desk. If Howard had been here, I wouldn't have hesitated to ask him to take another turn by Evans's. I wouldn't have minded suggesting I do it myself. But Howard wasn't here. At this hour even the guys in Howard's house were asleep. Professional courtesy required that one officer check in with him whose suspect was about to be grilled. A year ago, a month ago, I wouldn't have thought twice about overlooking that courtesy, knowing Howard would understand. But now . . . It was one thing for Howard to feel he was a step beneath me in our ultimate quest for Chiefdom; it was another for me to close a murder case by filching the information from his suspect.

Still, I needed to know about Lois Palmerston. And I was too keyed up to wait till morning.

I checked Howard's desk for Evans's address and left Howard a note, hoping he would understand.

I stopped by the dispatcher and gave him my destination. Dropping in on Leon Evans at three in the morning was definitely something to be done in a squad car. I didn't want to be mistaken for part of one of his other businesses.

I pulled the car out of the lot and headed down University Avenue toward San Francisco Bay. As I drove along the empty street with even the fast-food places and gas stations dark, I wished that I had asked Howard more about Leon Evans. That reticence, too, was due to the awkwardness of our new statuses. When we were both patrol officers, we had discussed every case and each piece of evidence, each clever deduction, what stymied us, what irritated, and what schemes we had to work around those obstacles. We had helped each other think, and we'd helped set the schemes in operation. Sometimes we'd gotten so involved in the other's case that it was hard to separate out who did what. But now, Howard seemed protective of his narcotics cases; he seemed to be saying "a poor thing, but mine own." Hoping that feeling would pass with time, I had kept my distance. Maybe it would pass, but right now I would have felt a lot better knowing if Leon Evans were violent or crazy. If he was

running his own show here in Berkeley, or if he was being
watched not only by his own lackeys but by those of his
bosses.

I pulled up in front of the address I had gotten from
Howard's file. It was a two-story fourplex painted a red
so bright that it shone even under the subdued street
lights. Raised in relief on the stucco above each window
was what appeared to be an arch-shaped stucco rope with
its apex celebrated in a bow. It had been a common type
of decoration when these buildings were built in the
twenties and thirties. Here, against the crimson stucco,
the rope was blue, the bow gold.

As I opened the squad car door, lights went off in the
lower-left-hand unit. Evans's address listed both the
lower and upper left apartments. I tried to remember
what calls we had had from this street, but West Berkeley
was a long way from Telegraph, my former beat, and
unless the calls down here had been something particularly unusual, I wouldn't have heard of them. I slipped
my purse strap over my shoulder, checking to make sure
the zipper across the top of the purse was open and my
gun handy. I stepped out into the deserted street.

The doors to all four units were in the center of the
building, with those leading to the stairs in the middle,
and the ones to the first floor units besides them facing
each other. The doors were bright green, the frames pur-
ple. The building looked as if Evans had gotten a starter's
painting kit and was determined to use every color. I
knocked. Through the front window a dim light was visible, as if someone was watching television with the lights
off.

The door to Evans's lower flat opened. The man in
front of me was almost as tall as Howard, very dark, and
very muscular, and must have weighed close to three
hundred pounds. He looked like a dictionary illustration
of "ominous."

"Police," I said. "I'm here for Leon Evans."

"Mr. Evans is asleep."

"I'll wait while he gets up."

"It's late."

"I said I'll wait."

The door shut. The air was heavy. It would probably start to rain again soon.

In a minute the door opened again. Mr. Ominous jerked his head to the right. I walked around him and into the darkened front room. It was the next room, the dining room of the lower flat, that the television light had come from. The set was in the middle of the archway separating the two rooms. A sofa sat opposite it. From the one large indentation, it was clear that this was the guard's post. To the right was a circular metal staircase that had been added. The guard nodded toward it. Keeping my head still, I took a final glance around the room, then climbed the stairs.

The room I emerged in looked like an Indian sari showroom. Silk was everywhere: it curtained the windows; it covered the sofas. Silk paintings adorned the walls. Thin strips of silk hung like beads in the archway between this and the front room, creating only a symbolic division. Now I recalled what I'd heard about Leon Evans. He was not the stereotypical drug dealer. No childhood in the ghetto for him. No up by his bootstraps, or "his nose hairs" as Howard had put it. Leon Evans was the son of two lawyers. He had grown up in a house like Ralph Palmerston's high in the hills. He'd gone through Berkeley High School, and two years at the University of California, when he decided to find himself in Thailand, India being somewhat passé as a spiritual mecca by then. What his spiritual experiences were in the Far East were anyone's guess, but what he'd found was obvious. And he'd made a lot of money selling it in the three years that he'd been back in Berkeley. Three years was a long time for a flamboyant drug dealer to stay on the outside, but

Evans not only had street smarts, but was the son of
lawyers.

Once I got over the effect of the silk, I realized that to
the riches of the East, Evans had added the state of the
art of the West. He must have had every piece of electronic equipment on the market. Without turning my
head I could see three televisions—a console, a mouse-
sized model, and a television–alarm clock (in case he
should forget to watch something on one of the others?).
There were two cordless phones, a videocassette recorder,
piles of stereo equipment, digital clocks, computer key-
boards, and a vibrating chair with headphones. On the
coffee table were three copies of *Digital Audio* magazine.

Evans himself was a small, dark man. He could have
passed as an Indian, or a light-skinned black (and perhaps he did at times), but his record listed him as white.
Looking at him, I remembered how tiny he had seemed
next to Howard.

"Remember me?" I asked.

He stared a moment. At three-fifteen he looked wide
awake. Howard had had him at the station yesterday
morning. He'd been out to bug him in the afternoon.
When did this man sleep? "The cop," he said.

"Right, the one you hollered at outside the station. We
don't like that attitude."

He shrugged, leaving unsaid, "So sue me!"

"You put Detective Howard in an awkward position."

"Ah, so sorry."

"We've got our code, Evans. Now Detective Howard
owes me, you understand? You can make up for that."

Again the shrug.

"I need some answers, some easy ones."

He turned his attention back to the television screen.

"This doesn't seem to be getting through to you," I
said. "Let me make it so you can understand. I'm offering
you the easy way out. You have something I want. You

can give it to me; I can tell Detective Howard, and he's off the hook. And, Mr. Evans, you're off the hook."

"Are you suggesting that Howard would harass me?"

"I'm suggesting that you tell me what I want to know."

He motioned me to the sofa cushion next to him. I couldn't see his guards. There could have been two or half a dozen standing behind the drapes of silk throughout the room. Or perhaps they were in the next room, observing us on closed-circuit television. "I'll stand."

He looked back at the television screen. It showed a Charlie Chan movie.

"Sam Nguyen," I said. "A drug deal five years ago."

He continued to stare at the screen. "I was out of the country five years ago."

I glanced around the room, hoping to discover something I could use as leverage—an artifact that might have been smuggled in, one that I could claim suspicion of, but there was nothing but electronic beeps and hanging silk. There wouldn't be; if there had been, Howard would have made use of it this afternoon, and Evans would certainly have it out of sight by now. What tack could Howard not have tried?

Now I did sit on the sofa. "Mr. Evans, I'm going to be straight with you. You are a very intelligent man. You may have been out of the country five years ago, but I'm sure you know everything that's gone on in the drug scene here for the last ten years or more. You're too thorough not to know your background."

"Why should I be interested in drugs?" His words were flat, as if just for the record.

"Let us say if you were to know about drugs. If you perhaps had an academic interest in the Berkeley drug scene. Most people who went to school here do."

The television switched to a commercial. I jerked my head toward it.

"What's the matter, you never seen a sales pitch before?"

"It hadn't occurred to me the movie wasn't on tape."

Now he stared at me, his thin lips stretched into a deliberate smile. "You, a police officer. It's dangerous for you to make assumptions."

"It's only on the little things."

He stared directly at me. His eyes were very dark, sunk deep. "There are no little things."

At three-fifteen I didn't need philosophical aphorisms. I also didn't want a veiled condemnation of my work. "What I am asking you for, Mr. Evans, is information that is of no importance to you."

"And what are you offering for that?"

"Good faith."

He laughed.

I took a long breath, forcing back the anger of the last few hours, making myself concentrate on this interchange alone. "Good faith may not seem like much, but then again, I'm not asking you for much."

"What exactly is your good faith worth? Are you going to good faith Howard off my tail? Are you going to good faith him out of here at the crack of dawn?"

I hesitated. I could ask Howard to lay off awhile. But Evans would use the time to move drugs and to dangle them in Howard's face. "I am a Homicide officer. No amount of good faith is going to keep you out of jail if you kill someone, but, Mr. Evans, you are engaged in a dangerous line of work. There have been a lot of drug-connected murders lately. The odds are that even someone as smart as you is likely to come to our attention sooner or later. Perhaps your employees will make a mistake, perhaps one of your customers may get himself killed right after he leaves here. Or maybe you'll just have bad luck. Whatever, a pleasant memory of you would encourage me to listen to your story just a smidgeon more sympathetically than I might if I could only recall you forcing me to spend days hunting for information that you can give me in three minutes."

He sat unmoving. No silk hangings shifted in the room. Somehow the absence of any appearance of violence was more ominous than guards with automatics in their hands.

"There are legal implications—"

"This has nothing to do with legalities."

The movie came back on the set. Evans looked toward it, then seemed to jerk his attention back to me. I wondered if he was on something or a combination of drugs. I wondered how long before the balance shifted, before his mellow, bantering mood slid into anger, or to sleep.

"Tell me what you're after," he said.

"There was a drug deal five years ago. Twenty-five thousand dollars down, more or less."

"It'd have to be a lot more to stand out. Twenty-five thousand is peanuts."

"Maybe the names of the people involved will bring it into focus." When he didn't reply, I said, "Sam Nguyen?"

"No," he said quickly. "There's no Asian ring in Berkeley. You should know that."

"Nguyen's in it with whites. Lois Palmerston, or as she was known then, Lois Burk?"

"No."

"Adam Thede?"

"No." His answers were coming quicker.

"Nina Munson? Jeffrey Munson?"

"No."

"Carol Grogan?"

"No."

I took a breath. "Cap Danziger?"

He hesitated.

"Cadillac salesman," I prompted.

"Oh yeah. I bought a couple of cars from him."

"I don't care about the cars, just the drugs."

He smiled that thin, stretched smile again. "Then, baby, you don't care. With Danziger I've only dealt in steel."

I sat for a moment trying to decide whether Evans was being honest with me. Could he not know any of them? Could they not be involved in drugs? If they had even the slightest connection with the Berkeley drug scene or the San Francisco or Oakland scenes, Evans would have made it his business to know. "Look," I said, "these people put up the twenty-five thousand dollars. Lois Palmerston handled it. Then her husband, who she married later, started going after them."

Evans's eyebrows narrowed. "Why would he do that?"

"You tell me."

"You're saying the group of them pulled the deal before this Palmer woman married the guy, then, all of a sudden, he's all hot about it and starts gunning for her partners?"

"Right."

"Don't make sense. You get your shipment; you sell your shipment; you get your money and you split. It's not like a marriage. It's a one-night stand."

I got up. "I hope you're being straight with me."

"Baby, you don't even know what you're talking about. If you were anyone but a cop, I'd have you tossed out of here for wasting my time."

"Yeah, but I am a cop."

20

The streets were empty as I drove back to the station.
Even the radio had only one squeal. At three-thirty on a
rainy October morning, Berkeley's criminals were lying
low. As I had earlier, I considered going home. But it
was too late to bother now. I wouldn't get there till four.
As wired as I was, it would take me an hour to get to
sleep. And then I'd spend the rest of the day trying to
wake up. I parked the squad car in the lot and headed
upstairs.

Dillingham, the night watch desk man kept the
watch's box of three dozen doughnuts. "Can I buy one
from you?" I asked.

"You can *have* one, Smith. A promotion gift from us,
like a gold watch. Even the same shape. We've still got
two jellies."

I barely knew Dillingham. My reputation had certainly
spread. Taking the doughnut, I headed to my desk. From
habit I checked my IN box and Howard's, but, of course,
nothing had changed since two-thirty. Then I sat, took a
bite of the doughnut, and considered the fiasco of my
night. If elimination is gain, then there might be some
value. But the only person who had really gained was
Leon Evans. I owed him, and in a more subtle way, Howard owed him. That had never been mentioned, but both
of us knew that he was Howard's suspect; it was the

mantle of Howard's investigation that covered my conversation with Evans.

I had no doubt that Evans had been telling me the truth. There was no reason for him not to. And there was a lot of reason for him to cooperate with me (and, by implication, with Howard) on this unimportant issue. The next time Howard rousted him out of bed at eight in the morning, Evans would remind him.

But what about the things I hadn't asked him? He knew Cap Danziger. And Sam Nguyen? Thinking back on his reaction when I'd asked about Sam, it was too quick a no. If Leon Evans had bought a Cadillac or two from Cap, then he knew Sam Nguyen. Cap himself told me that Sam was the draw at Trent Cadillac. So why hadn't Leon Evans mentioned at least knowing *of* Sam? Was it a normal reluctance to give the police anything? Or was his connection with Sam Nguyen somehow outside the law? Not drugs, but some other illegal pursuit?

If not drugs, what? What were Sam Nguyen, Lois Palmerston, and the Shareholders involved in? What was it that Lois could buy, smuggle, or steal that would make the investment so alluring that Carol Grogan would take a second mortgage on her house? Whatever the scheme it must have had a high probability of good return. Was it smuggling? Had Lois Palmerston used her trips with Ralph to bring in diamonds or currency? As much as the idea appealed to me, particularly the part about Ralph's being used as cover, it didn't hold. Lois had gotten the twenty-five thousand dollars before she had even met Ralph. At that time she wasn't traveling anywhere.

Blackmail? I found it even harder to believe that in the three months after Lois's arrival in Berkeley, she had found five people, three of them strangers, to blackmail.

So, if not blackmail, smuggling, or drugs, what? And why had Ralph Palmerston been so angry with Sam Nguyen the day he died? I leaned back in my chair. Why had Ralph been screaming at him?

* * *

"Jill, Jill! Wake up." Howard was shaking me. "What are you doing here? I know your apartment's not much but—"

"Howard?" It took me a moment to realize where I was.

"Come on, Jill. You've got five minutes to Detectives' Morning Meeting. And Jill"—he grinned—"you've got jelly on your face."

Before I realized it, I'd whipped my tongue out and licked the jelly off the side of my mouth. "Howard," I said, "what are your plans this morning?"

"I don't know. Why?"

"You weren't headed to see Leon Evans, were you?"

"No. Why?"

"Well, I hope this isn't going to screw up anything for you, and I should have asked you before—I left a note in your IN box—if it hadn't been three in the morning—"

"Jill! What are you talking about?"

"I went to Evans's place last night, this morning, actually. I needed some inside knowledge of the drug scene five years ago. I needed to know if my suspects were involved. I knew Evans would be able to tell me."

Howard took a breath. It was a moment before he said, "What did you use as leverage?"

"That I was in Homicide. I told him it would be good for me to think fondly of him." Howard didn't comment. I said, "I know it's got to reflect on you. He'll get what he can out of you for it."

He nodded. Looking at his watch, he said, "Three minutes. You'd better wash up before the meeting."

"Okay." I started to the door.

"Jill."

I turned.

"You've got jelly on your lapel, too."

"Damn." I headed down the hall to the ladies' room. Howard hadn't reacted as he would have a year ago. He hadn't said it was understandable that I questioned Evans, okay that I hadn't consulted him. My problem with Howard had always been his making too much of an effort to help me, even when it meant endangering his own career. If I had been talking to Jackson, or Eggs, or any of the other detectives, the restrained reaction Howard had shown would have been no more than I'd expected. Had I taken greater advantage of Howard than I'd realized?

I headed back down the hall, slipping into the meeting room just before Inspector Doyle. Doyle glanced at me and then looked away. I slumped into the chair next to Howard and wished I'd thought to get a cup of coffee.

The meeting was mercifully short. There was a training film afterward, on blood subgroups, I think. When the lights went on, I felt an elbow in my ribs, poking me awake. I looked at Howard before I realized the elbow was on my other side. From there Clay Jackson winked at me.

It was too early for Trent Cadillac to be open, but not so early that Jake Trent couldn't be up. In my office I dialed his home number.

"Yeah?"

"Mr. Trent, this is Detective Smith, Berkeley Police Department."

"You again? Don't you ever sleep? First you call me at midnight, now it's the crack of dawn."

"It'll just take a minute."

"Yeah, sure."

"You remember I asked you about Ralph Palmerston's scene with Sam Nguyen?"

"I remember, I remember. I told you all I know."

"What I didn't ask you was what was Nguyen's reaction. Did he look angry?"

"Lady, I don't know. He was racing out the door. He had his back to us."

"You couldn't guess from the hunching of his shoulders, or the way he walked?"

"Like I said, he was almost out the door. He was in a big hurry. He only went four or five steps. If they were different from his regular steps, I couldn't tell you."

"Why was he rushing?"

"Got me. Maybe he didn't want to deal with Palmerston."

"Why would that be?"

"Don't know."

"Any idea?"

"No."

"One more thing, Mr. Trent."

"Lady, I'm still in bed. I haven't even taken a leak yet."

"Cap Danziger—"

"Oh, geez. Danziger's not hiding behind Sam again, is he?"

"Why do you say that?"

"Forget it."

"What's going on between Cap Danziger and Sam Nguyen?"

"Look, I can't tell you that. I've got some loyalty to my men, even Danziger. He brings me a lot of Society trade."

"He also seems to bring you a lot of headaches."

"So he's not the most reliable guy on the floor. His paperwork . . . Geez, you'd think a college man would be able to get a loan application form done in a week. And his check-in calls. I told him, you got to keep up with the customers so when they think of trading in they think of you. But could he bother with those calls? They're bread and butter. I told him. I . . . he's been with the dealership five years on and off. He and Sam started together before I bought the place. He's screwed up a few times. I've fired him a few times. I've hired him back a few times."

"Why?" When he didn't answer, I asked, "Because his friend Sam Nguyen wanted you to?"

"Yeah. So? Sam's good for business."

And, I thought, Cap's indebted to Sam, or vice versa. "How did Danziger screw up?"

"Paperwork. Nothing up your line."

"Paperwork covers a lot of possibilities."

"Yeah, well, that's all I can say."

I hesitated, then decided to go with my original line of questioning. "Why was Cap Danziger talking to Ralph Palmerston?"

"I'd like to think he was buttering his bread."

"And *do* you think that?"

He didn't answer.

"Mr. Trent?" When he still didn't answer, I reminded him, "This is police business."

"Okay. I'll tell you. There's what we call the 'sales look.' It's sort of the 'you and me, buddy' look, the 'pat on the back' look, if you know what I mean."

"Right."

"Well, Danziger didn't have that look."

"Was he angry?"

"No. But I'll tell you, that was the only time I've seen Danziger look scared."

"Do you know why?"

"No. Mr. Palmerston didn't say. He was too caught up with Nguyen. I figured whatever happened between him and Danziger he'd forgotten, and I wasn't going to remind him, that's for sure."

"What about Danziger? What did he say?"

"I didn't ask him. To tell you the truth, lady, I forgot about that until you asked. Now, listen, before you think of any more 'last things,' I got stuff to do."

"Sure. Thanks for your help, Mr. Trent."

"Don't mention it. But look, don't call again, either, huh?" He hung up.

Pereira was standing behind me. "These aren't Cadillac hours, Jill," she said, grinning. "You look like you had a long night."

"I did. Where's Howard?"

"He was heading for a squad car when I saw him. But listen, let me tell you what I've got." Ignoring Howard's chair, she settled atop his desk, pulled out the lower drawer, and propped her feet on it. "It's the article on Lois Palmerston's breakfast party from the *Chronicle*. I mentioned it to you yesterday."

I nodded. "Breakfast?"

"Probably that's why it got the write up. It's not the usual cocktail party or dinner. It was after"—Pereira glanced at the Xerox in front of her—"one of the dinner dances for the mayor's campaign to save the cable cars."

"Five years ago?" I asked, feeling more awake.

"Close to it. A couple of months less."

"So what does it say?

"Actually, it's just a mention in the Society column—'And for those serious night owls there was Lois Burk's gourmet vegetarian breakfast at her home in Pacific Heights, where the sun rose over tofu and sprouts that even the most convinced carnivore would have loved.' "

"Does it name the carnivores?"

"No."

"But still, a gourmet vegetarian breakfast? How many places cater that type of meal?"

"A few would."

"But, Connie, why would Lois choose that type of meal? Not everyone is crazy about vegetarian food. People who are up all night want bacon and eggs. The reason," I said, now completely awake, "that Lois would do that is because she knew Adam Thede, and vegetarian breakfasts are what he makes."

"So?"

"So, besides investing five thousand dollars with Lois, Thede cooked for her affairs."

Turning, Pereira shoved Howard's IN box to one side and leaned back against the wall.

"What else did you find?" I demanded.

"I could have gotten the whole file on social climbing —it seems that someone compiled it a few years ago—but I didn't think it would deal with Lois Palmerston. It was before her marriage."

"Five years ago?"

"I think so."

"Was the person who compiled it a librarian?"

"I don't know. My librarian didn't say, but it sounded like a professional job."

I sat back—gourmet vegetarian breakfasts, research on social climbing.

"Jill," Pereira said, "I've got something to show you." She was grinning. "You're not going to believe these."

I nodded. Adam Thede and Carol Grogan.

"Look, Jill!"

I glanced up. Pereira held a pair of clear plastic high heels with rhinestones on the straps and embedded in the heels. "Aren't they perfect?"

I must have looked confused, for she said, "Glass slippers, Jill. Cinderella wore glass slippers. I had to pay forty dollars for these—"

"Forty dollars!" I stared at the plastic shoes.

"Well, I couldn't be Cinderella in hiking boots. The point of a costume, Jill, is to capture the whole effect. It's the small touches, the things that the real character would take for granted, that make the disguise work."

I stared. "The disguise!"

"Huh?"

"Disguise. That's what Lois Palmerston was doing."

"What?"

"I've been banging my head against the wall trying to think of why five people would invest five thousand dollars each with Lois Palmerston. I thought it was drugs, or smuggling, or blackmail. But with none of those was there a reason why Ralph Palmerston would suddenly, five years later, hire a detective to find out about the members of the group, and then attack each one of them at the point where it would hurt most. It didn't make sense till now."

"What?"

But I was already up, purse in hand, headed for the door.

21

It was a question of which of the five I would get the story from. Adam Thede might have been easier. I had the feeling that, had I known what to ask, he would have bellowed out the whole tale yesterday morning when we stood with our backs against opposite walls in his restaurant office. Any other detective would have headed for Thede, but I wanted to hear the story from Cap Danziger. I still didn't know whether he or Sam Nguyen was "our friend at Trent Cadillac," but Cap had been keeping an eye on me, either to protect himself or Sam. And he would be well aware of what went on with Shareholders Five. For him I took a squad car.

Cap Danziger lived in Cadillac land, high up in the hills. To be more accurate, it was Mercedes, BMW, and Volvo wagon land, with a few stray sports cars and the occasional Japanese compact for a son or a daughter.

The house was a Tudor with probably four bedrooms and a living room twice the size of my whole apartment. I couldn't imagine Cap Danziger affording this. And I was right. By the door was an extra mailbox with a sign scotch-taped on it saying CAMPBELL DANZIGER—AROUND BACK.

I followed the walkway around the house, down the slope of the hillside, to a door that led to a basementlike room. There was no bell. I pounded.

From inside came a groan.

I pounded again, louder.

He was tying a thick terry cloth bathrobe as he opened the door. He stared at me. "Jill? What happened to you?"

"I've been up all night." If I hadn't suspected that he knew exactly what had gone on at Lois Palmerston's after I'd left him last night, I would have taken his expression for one of concern. Instead, to me, it showed a sleepy man trying to recall how much he should know. "Can I come in?"

"Oh, of course." He stepped back.

It was a tiny, twelve-foot-square room, with a ceiling that couldn't have been over six-and-a-half feet high—clearly an illegal unit. Against the back wall was a rumpled, blanketed double bed, against a side wall an armoire, and in the front corner a table with a hot plate. In the remaining wall was a door that couldn't have been more than eighteen inches wide. It had to lead to the world's smallest bathroom. I almost laughed when I remembered that I had worried about what this man would think of *my* apartment.

The room was dark. The only window was next to the door I had come through. There was nothing on the walls —no pictures, not even a calendar.

"I can see why you spend your evenings in the showroom," I said, leaning against the wall. There wasn't even a chair to sit on.

"It's cheap."

"And a good address. That's important, isn't it, Cap?"

He took a moment to assess me. Even dragged from bed with his sandy hair hanging over his eyes, he still looked appealing. I had to remind myself that this man had invited me out for the purpose of pumping me. While I was searching Lois Palmerston's house, he, doubtless, was calling Sam Nguyen or the other four Shareholders to relay what I'd told him.

"Do you mind if I dress?"

"After we talk."

"I thought this was—"

"It's business. Everything between us has been business, right?"

He didn't answer. He didn't have to.

"Shareholders Five. Tell me about it."

"I don't know anything about such a group."

Someone else—anyone unfamiliar with the facts—wouldn't have doubted him. "Okay, let's start with something easier. Ralph Palmerston picked up his car from your shop at one-thirty. He drove it home and put it in the garage. The garage has an automatic door. You can hear it go up and down inside the house. The garage door wasn't tampered with. So, that means that the damage to Ralph Palmerston's brake lines happened in the Trent shop."

Cap sat down on the bed. His expression was that of one listening to a very boring customer.

"There are five people involved with Lois Palmerston who gave her five thousand dollars each. Ralph Palmerston made it his business to revenge himself on all five. But you, Cap, were the only one who was in the shop when the brake lines were punctured. You were talking with Ralph Palmerston. And you looked scared."

"I told you I was with him. I told you I was there when he spotted Sam Nguyen."

"But he didn't spot Sam Nguyen, did he?"

"I said he did."

"Sam Nguyen was all the way across the room. Ralph Palmerston was going blind. He didn't drive because his sight was so bad. He wouldn't have spotted Nguyen across the room. He wouldn't have noticed anything across the room. You pointed out Sam, didn't you? What did you say—that Sam had criticized his car, how it was kept up, or how it was driven?"

"Why would I do that?"

Taking a breath, I made my choice between Cap and Sam.

"To distract Ralph Palmerston from you. What was he telling you? Was he suggesting that he was going to use his influence to get Jake Trent to fire you?"

Cap hesitated, but remained silent.

"Or was it more than that? A job, one particular job wasn't that important to you, was it? You could have gotten another job, sold cars at another dealership, in another city. As long as you were accepted in Society, you could always get a job, right?"

He still said nothing, but his silence had the look of acquiescence.

"It was that social acceptance where Ralph Palmerston was going to attack you, wasn't it? You told me how, yourself. He'd let them know that you broke the rules, that you made use of them for Lois. Now do you want to tell me about it, or shall I work it out?"

He hunched forward, the collar of his terry cloth bathrobe shifting up around his ears.

"Here or at the station?"

He sighed. "All right. It's not illegal. Actually, it didn't even start as a plan, it was just a game, with the five of us sitting around Adam's house after one of his parties, eating one of his stragglers' breakfasts. I think it was Carol's idea, not that it matters. She was complaining about needing money, about her ex-husband not paying support. And then out of the blue, she said, 'What I need is a rich husband.' Adam said something like, 'Where do you think you're going to find one?' Then there was some discussion about Adam inviting a better class of bachelors to his parties. And I said, that if you want to marry money, you have to go where it is—to the Society functions. Carol looked down at whatever combination of garments she'd thrown on, probably jeans and an ancient sweater, and said, 'Like this?' So then there was a discussion about how you have to look the part in order to even get past the door at the right affairs. You need the right address. You need to give the appearance of money. Somewhere in that banter Carol said, 'Well, why don't you bankroll me to marry a rich man? It'd be an investment, like a money market account only the payoff would be better.' We weren't serious then. It was late, we'd been drinking, partying. We were just toying with a fantasy."

So Cap *was* the fifth Shareholder. I shifted my weight to the other foot. "But you didn't bankroll Carol."

"No. I don't think Carol's ever quite forgiven me. I was the one that pointed out her deficiencies. She was local. Her father was a fireman, hardly top-drawer. She was divorced from a guy who could be bugging her for the rest of her life if he discovered she had a rich husband. It wouldn't be hard for any prospect to find that out. And that's not even taking into consideration her biggest drawback—two small kids. Physically, Carol was all right. She could have been made up well, and dressed well, but her personality. Well, let's just say that Carol can be too honest."

"So you thought of Lois."

"No. I didn't know Lois. Nina did. She said she had the perfect friend. Beautiful, an actress. From New York. She said she could get her out here."

"And then what happened?"

He sat up straighter. "You know this isn't illegal."

"I didn't say *this* was. What happened after the party?"

"Well, about a month passed. I'd really forgotten about the whole discussion, when Nina called me and said her friend was here. That pretty much forced our hands. We got together and talked about the project like it would really happen. Then we realized that we were going to need money for clothes, money to rent a suitable apartment, money for charitable contributions—Society charity functions are where a woman can be seen. We were going to need a lot of money."

"Five thousand each?"

"Right. It wasn't easy to come by. I had some money I'd inherited, but that five thousand wiped it out."

"And then you assigned tasks?"

He looked quizzical.

"You were the escort. Lois had to have an entrée into Society, someone acceptable, like you. Adam Thede catered. Nina"—I recalled the photo of the one white-on-white long dress on her wall, amongst the other pictures of brightly colored patchwork jackets—"Nina made Lois's wardrobe, Jeffrey got her the car, and Carol researched exactly how to social-climb."

Slowly, he nodded.

"What was the payoff?"

"Two thousand a year."

"Each?"

"Yes."

"Not bad."

"In the long run it wouldn't have been. But the first couple of years it was hard on most of us. Maybe not Adam, but on Carol, Nina, and me."

I didn't need Cap Danziger to tell me that this was the scheme Lois Palmerston had admitted to Ralph in that emotional moment when she and Ralph both thought he was going to die. And this was the one scheme to which Ralph would have reacted so violently. Any other deal where five people loaned his wife money, he might have had some qualms about. Had it been drugs, he doubtless would have objected; he was that type of man. Perhaps he would have presumed that Lois's evil companions had led her astray, but he probably would have accepted the fact that she had some responsibility. But not with this scheme, not with one to trick him into marriage. If he cared about his marriage, or about Lois; if he wanted to preserve the illusion that his wife loved him—and what dying man wouldn't—he *couldn't* consider her as anything but a pawn in the plot, a pawn who had come to love him after their marriage. He would have absolved her, but the restraint he'd shown to her would have exploded in his revenge against the cold-blooded plotters who had used his wife to make a fool of him. It was the only scheme that would have generated the intensity of revenge Ralph had had. And the most devastating manifestation of that revenge would have been aimed at the man who had dated Lois: Cap himself.

Cap Danziger was still sitting on the foot of his bed, his bathrobe tied loosely around his waist, his legs crossed.

"Why did you kill Ralph Palmerston?"

He jumped up. "I didn't kill him. Do you think I would tell you all this if I'd killed him?"

"You were at the repair shop."

"I was with Palmerston. I couldn't have been under the car. Don't you think Sam Nguyen would have found it odd for me to rush into the shop, push myself under the car he was working on, with an ice pick or something in my hand?"

"Maybe Sam left?"

"You know by the time Sam left I was with Palmerston. Jake Trent saw me there. How much more of an alibi do you want?"

"Well, then if you didn't kill him, who did? It had to be one of you five."

"Why one of us? Why not Lois?"

"Because, Cap, Ralph Palmerston wasn't threatening her."

He sat back on the bed. "Then I don't know. I really don't. I never wanted to think about it, and I haven't."

"But you've been in contact with the others, haven't you? You kept tabs on me for them."

He shrugged. "It wasn't unpleasant. We were all worried. You're bound to worry when you're a police suspect, no matter how innocent you are."

I took a guess. "You called in the complaint about me, didn't you."

Now he did look uncomfortable. "That had nothing to do with the murder. We just wanted to keep you from finding out about our scheme. It only made sense for me to call. I know how to get service from public representatives. That's one of the advantages of growing up in Society. You assume public servants will serve, and if you approach them right, they do."

"You did all this and you expect me to believe you don't know who killed Ralph Palmerston? It had to be one of you five."

He didn't answer. And as I waited for him to dress, I wondered if indeed it did have to be one of the five Shareholders, or if it could be the person who would have found puncturing Ralph Palmerston's brake lines no trouble at all.

22

I drove Cap Danziger back to the station. It gave me a perverse delight to glance in the rearview mirror and see him back there in the cage. I was beginning to have a real understanding of Ralph Palmerston's reaction. Suppose Cap Danziger had told me that Adam Thede or Nina Munson had coerced him into pumping me. Even knowing better, I would have wanted to believe him, just to salvage my self-respect. And that was in reaction to one evening, one kiss. How much greater would Ralph Palmerston's feelings have been after four years of marriage? And even more than any of the other suspects, he would have despised Cap Danziger. Cap had been his social equal, a man whom he probably had met, a man who had been Lois's escort—and how much more? Palmerston's revenge on Adam Thede destroyed his livelihood and his dreams. What had he planned for Cap Danziger?

I took Cap's statement, had him wait while it was typed. Another suspect I might have gotten coffee, but Cap Danziger I let sit empty-handed. Ralph Palmerston's reaction was seeming more and more understandable. When the statement was signed, I called a patrol officer to drive Cap Danziger home.

Howard was leaving the office as I walked in. He nodded but didn't stop. I started for the door, to call him back. Was he angry about my questioning Leon Evans last night, or was he just in a hurry? I was too tired to judge. So I sat staring at the door, willing someone to drop in so I could talk about the great break in my case. But no one came, and as I thought about it, the question arose: So what? What clue does that give you to who killed Ralph Palmerston? Are you any closer than before? All the Shareholders Five were involved in the scheme. And there was Sam Nguyen, who had started to work at the same time Cap Danziger did, who took Cap to lunch with him, whom Ralph Palmerston was screaming at, and who was not walking, but *racing* out the door of the repair shop.

The excitement that had sustained me since Cap Danziger's confession faded. Talking to him, taking his statement, waiting for it to be typed had consumed a lot of time. It was almost noon. I hadn't eaten anything but night watch's doughnut since the taco at dinner. What I needed was a meal, a decent meal. Even I couldn't face another jelly doughnut. And I wouldn't be hurt by a shower and clothes that didn't have salsa and jelly on them.

I signed out and drove along Martin Luther King Junior Way toward my apartment. At the corner of University Avenue, waiting for the lights to change, was a witch. I crossed with the traffic. At the next crosswalk, a tiny punk-rocker, two goblins, and a white rabbit made their way, giggling and waving at the cars. I had forgotten today was Halloween. Berkeley celebrated Halloween in a big way. If you walked into the East Bay MUD office to pay your water bill, you might be greeted by Cleopatra; in the grocery you could be checked out by an executioner. At the department those of us on patrol or in Details showed some restraint, but one year all the clerks had turned up in prison stripes.

I pulled up in front of the Kepple house. Perhaps Mr. Kepple would appear as Ebenezer Scrooge. But when I spotted him, he looked as he always did—a portly, sixty-ish, bald man wearing brown polyester pants and a wind-breaker. He was blowing leaves off his short driveway with an electric blower. Without asking, I knew that when he finished here, he would make his way along the path to the backyard and my flat, blower whirring like the dentist's air squirter. I was only pleased that I hadn't considered taking a nap.

I waved and headed for my door.

I'd half expected the apartment to be filled with the aura of Cap Danziger, but it just looked like home. Grabbing a robe, I headed for the shower.

As the hot water beat on my back, I pondered Cap Danziger and Sam Nguyen. Were they just friends—two elitists thrown together? Was that why Sam had used his influence with Jake Trent to get him to rehire Cap each time he fired him? Or was the bond between Sam and Cap more than mere friendship? Love? Not an outlandish thought, particularly in the Bay Area. But neither Cap nor Sam had given any indication of being gay. If not love, was the thing that linked them blackmail?

Blackmail? Which way? If Sam were threatening to expose Cap over . . . I had suspected Jeffrey Munson of being Lois's lover. It had been hard to picture Lois with Jeffrey. But it was easy to imagine her with Cap. So if Sam Nguyen had threatened to tell Ralph Palmerston about Cap and Lois, it would have given both of them very good reason to kill Palmerston before he found out and changed his will.

And the other way—Cap blackmailing Sam? I couldn't come up with anything that would have involved Ralph Palmerston.

But I could find out about both of them. I rinsed off the soap as fast as I could, whisked the towel around my body, headed for the closet, and grabbed a forest green T-shirt that said STINSON BEACH on it, turned it inside out, and put my jacket over it. I'd just have to remember not to take the jacket off. But I'd had practice at that. Putting back on the same slacks (miraculously unstained), I headed for Munsonalysis.

The receptionist looked up as I walked into the Munsonalysis office. On her desk the multitude of electronic devices sat neither blinking nor beeping.

"I'm here to see Jeffrey Munson. I'm with the police."

"He's not here now."

"When will he be back?"

"I don't know." There was no hostility in her voice. It was simply a statement of fact.

"Doesn't he usually give you a time he'll be back?"

"Usually, but he didn't today."

"Why not today?"

"He got a call, and he left."

"Who was the call from?"

There was a slight hesitation before she said, "I couldn't tell you."

"Yes, you could. It was a voice you recognized, wasn't it?"

She lowered her head. She looked like a demure Japanese doll.

"It was from his wife, wasn't it? From Nina?"

Now she looked up. Her expression—knowing, disgusted—was anything but demure. "Yes."

"Thanks."

Jeffrey's Porsche, with its radical-chic dented exterior, was parked in front of 1733 Gilroy Street. Nina's door was open. Through it I could see Jeffrey seated on the fainting couch, with the snapshots of Nina's white-on-white dress and her bright jackets behind him, and the clothes rack with the white painting overalls and the multitude of brightly patched garments next to him. In a beige-striped rugby shirt, tan cords, and tan running shoes, Jeffrey looked more akin to the whites than the brights.

I walked in, and starting on the offensive, said to him, "Cap Danziger called today, didn't he?"

It was Nina, seated at her work table across from him who said, "Yes."

Beside Jeffrey was the pile of jackets with the store labels on them that I had seen before. "Returned?" I asked.

"Yes," Nina said.

"What reason did the store owners give you?"

"They didn't. When you own a place, you don't have to explain. They just said they were returning them."

"Didn't you ask why?"

She sat a moment, looking small and dark against the brightly colored fabrics on the table behind her. "I knew why. I'd already talked to Adam, and to Carol. It was just a question of waiting to see what tack Ralph took with me. It could have been worse. This will pass. These jackets aren't fashion items. They don't go out of style. I'll sell them next year."

"Now that Ralph Palmerston is dead, you will. If he had lived, those stores would never have handled them."

"Maybe. But this isn't the only market. I could take them to L.A. It's inconvenient. But I could do it."

"Still, things are a lot easier for you now that Ralph's dead."

She looked straight at me, her brown eyes catching mine. "They are, but I didn't kill him. Why should I, after the fact?"

I could see that it would be a long time before I rattled her into revealing anything. Jeffrey Munson sat watching her. To him, I said, "But it's a different affair with you, isn't it? Ralph Palmerston knew that you worked for Von Slocum, the South African supplier. That's what you did five years ago to get the money to pay Lois, isn't it?"

"Listen, I don't need to answer questions from you." His hands tightened into fists.

"Maybe working for Von Slocum wasn't such a sacrifice."

He flushed.

"Maybe it wasn't your only South African deal."

His lips pressed together.

"It's like your Porsche—radical on the outside, Republican under the hood."

He slammed his fist into the couch. "I needed money fast. I didn't want to. I just couldn't think of any other way to get that kind of cash. But I've given more than that amount to groups working against apartheid since then." He looked toward Nina.

She said, "He did what he had to; I did what I had to. I had a necklace to sell."

"And you can live more cheaply?"

"Listen, she gets her quarter of the net from Munsonalysis, I see to that," Jeffrey insisted.

"That's right," Nina said. "Jeffrey's been fair to me."

I'd let him calm down too much. "To get back to Ralph Palmerston," I said, "Nina's right in saying that what Ralph planned for her, he did. But for you, Jeffrey, it was still coming, wasn't it? Ralph Palmerston penciled in the dates he carried out his well-prepared revenges—Adam Thede 9/26, Carol Grogan 10/12, Nina 10/25. But there was no date by your name. What was he going to do, leak to the newspapers that you'd worked for Von Slocum? Or was he just going to let the word out on the avenue, or with one or two protest groups?"

Jeffrey glanced at Nina, then said, "What difference would it make? The effect is the same. If he told one person, he might as well have painted it on my building wall, like graffiti."

"It would destroy your business, wouldn't it?"

"It would destroy me," he said quietly.

"But if you stopped him before the word got out, then it would be all right."

It was Nina who said, "It's never been all right for

Jeffrey, since the moment he made the decision to work for those bigots."

Ignoring that, I said, "Jeffrey, you know cars inside and out. It would have been easy for you to puncture the brake lines. It was an expert job, but you could have done it, couldn't you?"

"I didn't, dammit, I didn't." His voice was shaky; his hands were pressed together.

"It would have been so easy, Jeffrey. Two holes, and everything would be all right. You said Ralph Palmerston was a parasite; he wouldn't be missed."

"I didn't." His voice was lower.

"You said Lois was a parasite. Look at all you and Nina did for her. Nina took care of her in college. After college, you gave her a place to live. You brought her out here. You paid for that, right, Jeffrey?"

Slowly, he nodded.

"You spent weeks working on her car. How long did it take Nina to make her beautiful clothes? Nina sold her necklace. You endangered your business. You sold your soul for her, didn't you, Jeffrey?"

Nina seemed about to speak, but didn't.

Jeffrey just sat, but his fists were tight.

"Lois threw it all back in your face, didn't she? She told Ralph Palmerston about the deal you had. She gave him your names. She watched as he plotted his revenge."

"Dammit! Dammit!" Jeffrey was screaming. "Fucking bitch! She could have stopped him. Goddamn fucking bitch."

"Who killed him, Jeffrey? Was it Cap Danziger? Was he Lois's lover?"

I'd expected a shout of confirmation, or of outrage, but what I got was a muddled stare. The notion of Cap and Lois was clearly a new one for Jeffrey. I turned to Nina questioningly.

She took a breath. "Lois always had her choice of men. Why would she kill a rich 'parasite' for a penniless one?"

"Charm, love, sex?"

"Lois wasn't easily charmed."

Nina seemed certain, but that didn't mean Lois hadn't been having an affair with Cap; it just showed that Nina couldn't see any logic to it. But sensible, frugal Nina was not Lois.

Jeffrey's breath was still shallow, his face red. Nina's calm hadn't affected him at all.

"Sam Nguyen?" I demanded.

"Sam?"

"You worked as a mechanic when you arrived in Berkeley. You knew Sam then, right?"

"Yes. Everyone in the business knew Sam."

"What is Sam's racket, Jeffrey?"

"He's a good mechanic, the best."

"He's doing more than tuning engines. What is it, Jeffrey? Why are the drug dealers so interested in Sam Nguyen?"

"I don't know. I don't know." He looked panicked. "Sam made over cars, that's all."

Nina jumped up, rushed over to him, and put her arm around his shoulder. Jeffrey sighed. "It is all," she said.

Maybe it was all, I thought as I drove back to the station. I recalled Sam Nguyen standing in the repair shop and telling me "secret cargo space—no problem." He might deny any knowledge of what would go into those compartments, but we could probably haul him in on conspiracy the next time we busted one of his customers like Leon Evans. And once his business was common knowledge, once every police force kept an eye on his vehicles, the Leon Evanses of the world would keep away —or worse—lots worse.

But where did Sam Nguyen fit in with Shareholders Five?

23

The last time I had seen Carol Grogan, she had been dressed in a T-shirt and sweat pants, sitting amongst an avalanche of plastic trucks and blocks in her living room. But this afternoon, for a trip to the police station, she wore a tan wraparound skirt, plaid blouse with roll-up sleeves, stockings, and stacked heels—her library clothes. She had made a passing effort at makeup, but it wasn't the right effect for her unusual features. Rather than accenting their charm, it brought out their peculiarity. Her expression was anything but attractive as she sat down in the interview booth.

"Dustin and Jason get out of day care in an hour," she announced angrily.

"The more quickly you answer my questions, the earlier you can leave. Day-care centers don't turn children out on the street if their parents are a few minutes late."

"They charge extra. That's all I need right now."

"You gave Lois five thousand dollars. She was to pay you two thousand every year. Did she pay off on schedule?"

"It wasn't illegal."

"I'm not saying it was. I'd just be surprised if Lois kept her end of the deal."

"You and everyone else by now. Oh, the first year she was right there on time. The second year it was just a little late. But by the third year, it was six months late and a thousand dollars short. And this year, zip."

"Is that why you had her to dinner, to demand your money?"

"It's what I had in mind. But it didn't take long for her to convince me that I had no power to demand from. When I threatened to go to Ralph, she laughed. She said Ralph knew. He understood her part."

"Did you believe her?"

"Oh yeah. Lois had a way with men, particularly with Ralph Palmerston. After all, if he hadn't been so fascinated with her in the beginning, he could have hired someone to check into her background. It wouldn't have taken much to discover that there was nothing behind her fancy address and her Mercedes. But Ralph didn't do that. Even then, he didn't want to know. There was no reason he should want to know now."

That made sense. I asked, "Are you going to sell your house?"

She clutched the strap of the big imitation leather purse on her lap. Her mouth twitched. She seemed on the verge of tears. "If I can work it out with the holder of the second mortgage, I will. You know you can lose everything by not paying your second."

"But it's more than just selling a house, isn't it?"

She looked down at the purse.

I said gently, "You won't be able to get another house, will you?"

She didn't respond.

"And for all this you have Cap Danziger to blame." When she hesitated, I said, "And when you and your kids are jammed into a tiny apartment, Cap will marry Lois and live off the Palmieri Winery."

Her eyes closed. She seemed to be considering the premise.

"They've been having an affair, haven't they, Carol?"

Now she looked up. "If they were lovers, they wouldn't tell me."

"Your idea was for you to be the one to marry money, wasn't it?" I prompted.

Momentarily she looked surprised. "If Cap had listened to me, we wouldn't have had any problems. If I'd been married to Ralph Palmerston, I wouldn't have told him all my secrets when I heard he was going blind. Christ, if Lois didn't have any decency, at least she could have used some sense. I never thought she'd be so bubbleheaded. Cool, calm Lois. How could she do such a stupid thing?"

It wasn't what I would have expected of Lois either. But Lois hadn't said she had brought up the subject. She'd said Ralph asked her about her childhood, her boyfriends, her lovers, and her debts. Her debts were an odd inclusion in the otherwise emotional subjects. Why would Ralph have asked not *if* she had debts, but *whom she owed,* unless he already knew she owed money? Had someone told Ralph about Shareholders Five? Had that been the initial reason he hired Herman Ott—to find out if his wife was involved with the five?

Certainly none of the Shareholders would have told Ralph. Only someone who wanted to get even with one of them would. Someone like Sam Nguyen.

By the time Carol Grogan left, it was well after five o'clock. I had no address for Sam Nguyen. It was Saturday, and Trent Cadillac was closed by now. The only place I knew that Sam might be was the Bien Hoa restaurant.

I signed out and headed for my car three blocks away. At dusk, with stores emptying out and afternoon parties ending, the sidewalks were filled with clowns, ballerinas, hobos, and robots.

I crossed the street and hurried down the block past the child-care center with its alluring white curb. Inside the gate, an angel holding her mother's hand walked toward the street. Two small, painted faces looked out the window hopefully. Costumed party-goers straggled across crosswalks, as if protected from harm by their sheets and spangles.

I could picture Sam Nguyen telling Ralph Palmerston about Shareholders Five. In my mind, I could see the short, dark-haired mechanic in his white overalls, leaning toward the tall, gray-haired Palmerston. I could see Palmerston's blue eyes with the same shocked expression they had had in death. And I could imagine Palmerston finding a detective to check out Sam Nguyen's bizarre story.

I unlocked my car door, climbed in, and started the engine.

But how would Sam have known about Shareholders Five? He and Cap Danziger had been friends. Had Cap told him? Had he laughed about his great scheme? But then why would Sam expose him?

I pulled into traffic.

Then it came to me—friendship and good intentions were a rare commodity in Lois Palmerston's associates. And just as Ralph Palmerston had not been doing "something nice" for the Shareholders, it made sense that Cap and Sam were not friends now. Maybe they had never really been friends, although, according to Jake Trent, Sam Nguyen had intervened to save Cap's job on more than one occasion. I'd have to ponder that later. But what I could be sure of was that if Sam and Cap weren't friends, Cap would not have revealed the Shareholders Five scheme to Sam. Damn! How did he find out, if not from Cap?

I slammed on the brakes, barely missing a devil's pitchfork.

Finding Sam Nguyen at the Bien Hoa and forcing him to tell me was a long shot. But it was my only shot.

It took me half an hour to make my way into Oak-

land's Chinatown, an area of hole-in-the-wall cafés and
larger, plastic-fronted restaurants. Ten years ago it had
been almost totally Chinese, but now the Chinese restaurants were interspersed with Thai, Cambodian, and Vietnamese. Refugee agencies worked out of storefronts. In
the daytime it was crowded with old women in loose
batik garments, children in bright polyester jumping the
gap from their ancestral lives to American ways. But after dusk, urban Oakland was like the inner city anywhere.

The Bien Hoa Vietnamese Restaurant was one store-
front wide. There had to be more than fifty customers
crowded together inside. The steam from the kitchen
filled the room and opaqued the windows.

I made my way between tables to the formica counter
at the back where the cash register sat. Before the small,
young woman behind it could speak, I showed her my
shield.

Warily, she said, "Yes?"

I would have to approach my need for Sam Nguyen's
address obliquely. "Sam Nguyen, the mechanic, eats
lunch here, doesn't he?"

"Sam Nguyen." She smiled, then looked even more
nervous.

"It's okay," I said. "Sam Nguyen told me he eats lunch
here."

She nodded.

"Every day?"

"Every day he works."

Good—every workday. "Does he come at the same
time every day?"

"Oh yes. Always he arrives here at twenty minutes
after one o'clock. We have his masseuse waiting. We are
preparing his special dishes. We have his special dishes
ready when he is relaxed—after his masseuse. We are
waiting for him. He would not disappoint."

I smiled. This restaurant sounded like Sam's second

home. If anyone knew where his real home was, they would be here. "This week, has Sam Nguyen been here at twenty after one every workday?"

"Oh yes, every day."

"Thank you." I made a show of turning toward the door, stopped suddenly, and turned back. "There's one more thing I need to ask him. Can you give me his address?"

She shrank back. "I do not know that."

"Where does he live? Near here?"

She shook her head. "I see him only at lunch. He drives here in a big car, I do not know from where."

Obviously my approach had not been oblique enough. Behind me the restaurant had grown quiet. I considered pressing harder, but I knew I'd get nothing out of this close immigrant community. By now someone had probably moved silently out the back door and was running to warn Sam. Even if I could get his address, he would be gone.

But maybe I could find his other friends. "Who does Sam eat with?"

She brightened. "Sometimes he brings a man, with light hair, in a light suit. A tall man. From where he works."

Cap Danziger. "Recently?"

"Not so much. More times two, three years ago."

That fit my theory that they were no longer really friends. "Anyone else?"

"A woman. She comes with the man two times."

Carol Grogan? "What did she look like?"

"Light hair, tall, thin—like a model."

"Was her hair caught in combs at the sides of her head?"

"Yes, yes." She nodded enthusiastically.

Lois Palmerston! "You said they came two times—when?"

"One time was last month. One was before."

"Thanks." I turned and walked back to my car smiling. So Sam Nguyen didn't need to know about Shareholders Five. He only needed to see Cap Danziger with the young wife of a rich customer and put two and two together. To Cap and Lois the lunches—meals in a crowded, hardly romantic Vietnamese restaurant—would have been innocent affairs, or at least occasions when they thought they were disguising any mutual attraction. But Sam Nguyen would not have been fooled. Then he would have told Ralph Palmerston his wife was having a fling. And Ralph would have hired Herman Ott not to look into Shareholders Five, but to find out if his wife was unfaithful. That was exactly the sleazy type of case Ott would be chosen for. And in checking out Lois and Cap, Herman Ott would have come upon Shareholders Five.

It all fit. It explained why Cap Danziger would kill Ralph Palmerston.

But Cap had an alibi for the time of the sabotage to the car. It was Sam Nguyen who had had the opportunity to puncture the brake lines. And Sam Nguyen had no motive. He'd already told him his wife could be having an affair; there was no point in killing him.

24

It was just after eight when I got to Pereira's apartment. Connie opened the door. Her blond hair curled around her face. A gold tiara sat atop her head. And her ball dress, a scooped-necked white bouffant with pink roses on the hip flounces, hung down to the floor. When she stepped back, the hoop skirt swayed and I could see her plastic shoes—her glass slippers.

"You really look like Cinderella, Connie," I said as I dragged my own costume over my head.

"And you," she said, looking at my green monk's robe, "are an interesting Fairy Godmother. Here's your pumpkin and your magic wand."

"It's going to take more than a magic wand to get all of your dress into my car."

We made our way out, Pereira navigating her hoop skirt, me carrying the pumpkin and wand. When she finally squeezed the hoop and the dress into the car and was propped against the seat, clutching both sides of the hoop so I could reach the gear stick, she said, "What about Howard's costume? Did you discover what it is?"

"I have an idea."

"Well?"

"It seems like Howard has been spending an awful lot of time with Leon Evans in the last few days, doesn't it? He had Evans at the station yesterday morning. He was at Evans's apartment for a couple hours in the afternoon. He's complained about him to all of us. And by now we all know who Leon Evans is and what he looks like, right?"

Connie grinned. "So you think he's coming as Leon Evans?"

"It fits. I was sure his disguise would be connected to something important to him. Evans symbolizes his promotion."

Connie's grin grew wider. "I can hardly wait to see Howard in skintight red silk pants."

"Hi! Wow!" What appeared to be a mound of leaves opened Howard's door. At closer inspection, the leaves were pasted to a sheet that hung over an egg-shaped frame. Halfway down the front there was a sign saying COMPOST HEAP. It had to be Howard's roommate Ellis, a horticulture student at Cal. He was looking at Pereira.

Ellis stood back, his dark eyes staring out holes between leaves as Pereira maneuvered the hoop skirt in through the door. Between Ellis's ovoid pile and Connie's skirt, they filled the entire entryway. Clutching my pumpkin, I followed them in.

Across the room I spotted Howard, red curls snapping out beneath his uniform hat. He wasn't Leon Evans. He wasn't even close. He wasn't in costume at all. He was just in his old patrol officer uniform. I couldn't believe it —after our bet and all his goading, he'd copped out— literally—on the whole thing. Furious, I started toward him.

He turned, facing me. He wasn't even Howard! He was just a tall guy with a red wig and a mask dressed in the khaki uniform. I tried to place the body—one of the guys at work? One of Howard's other roommates? But I couldn't tell.

The house was a huge brown-shingled affair, with six bedrooms upstairs and a balcony that led to them overlooking the living room. It was suitable only for six single guys and as many roommates as they chose to have, or one very large and wealthy family. Now the living room was packed. There had to be a hundred people here. Music bounced off the walls. In the middle of the room, cleared for a dance floor, ghosts were shaking their sheets, a cigarette girl leaned on a magician, and Howard danced with Howard.

"Drink?" the front end of a horse asked.

"Sure," Pereira answered.

"Gangway, gangway," the half-horse called, leading us across the floor.

As I passed by the pair of dancing Howards, I realized that the Howard with its back to me was a woman, a black woman, who had been with the last training class for two months before deciding to get a master's degree instead. She'd said it was bad enough to be a six-foot woman without being a cop, too.

"Mind if I stash this here?" I asked, plopping my pumpkin on the food table. To Pereira, I said, "Why didn't you get me a plastic pumpkin, one of the ones with the little tin handles?"

"Verisimilitude. It's important."

"Maybe you overdid it on that. Tell me about verisimilitude two hours from now when you're still driving that dress around the dance floor."

"I'd better be on the dance floor. In this, I can't sit without taking up four chairs."

The food ran mostly to cold cuts, chips, and dips—healthy stuff for me. I made myself a ham-and-cheese sandwich with the hotest mustard on the table and even a slice of lettuce for good measure and chomped down.

A gorilla asked Pereira to dance.

"Hey, Smith, you trying out for the monastery?" It was Clayton Jackson in his promised Oakland Raiders shirt. "You've met my wife, Yvonne, and my kids?"

"Hi, Yvonne." I looked at the four Raiders-shirted

Jackson children. They ranged from eight to fifteen years old. "I didn't think kids would enjoy a party like this."

Yvonne laughed. "Maybe not. We *know* what they'd like to be doing, especially this one." She patted the oldest boy on the shoulder. He grimaced. "They're here where we can keep an eye on them."

The kids spotted the refreshment table and crowded around the pretzels and chips.

Across the room I saw yet another Howard. "How many of these Howard impersonators are there?" I asked Clay.

"Enough to make a basketball team from what I've seen."

"Did Howard—the real Howard—know about them?"

"Not before now. Way I heard it one of his roommates kept him upstairs till they all got here."

"I wonder if he caught on right away," Yvonne said.

"Honey, you can't miss them—all that red hair, and that tall," Clay said. "Hey, man, you stocking up for the winter there," he said to his oldest son. "Leave a mouthful for the rest of the people."

"What I meant," Yvonne said with a trace of annoyance, "is that we all recognize them as Howards, but Howard doesn't see himself from a distance. He doesn't look up at himself, and he sure doesn't see himself from the back."

"What did he say?" I asked.

A Howard put a platter on the far end of the table. But this was no Howard like the others I'd just seen. This was the real Howard. I'd been wrong though; he wasn't dressed as Leon Evans. He wore a gray business suit, with a white shirt, and a narrow red tie—like Chief Larkin's gray suit and never-changing narrow red tie. I had known Howard would come as someone or something significant to him. How had I gotten sidetracked on Leon Evans and missed a disguise so obvious as the culmination of his own ambitions—Chief of Police?

"Oh my God," I said, "no wonder I couldn't find out anything about your costume."

Howard grinned.

"It's not like I didn't try either. I checked your messages ever time I was in the office. I went to the costume store. They searched through all their records."

Howard laughed.

"I even called the French consulate to see where you could get a de Gaulle disguise."

Howard laughed harder.

"I finally decided you'd be a silk-clad Leon Evans."

Howard was nearly doubled over. Between fits of laughter, Jackson was explaining the bet to Yvonne.

To Clay, I said, "Think how guilty you're going to feel about this display when you see me hobbling into the station after trudging miles from my car."

"Keeps you in shape, Smith," he said.

"Clayton doesn't need to be so smug," Yvonne put in. "He's never gotten a garage."

"You guys can visit." Howard was only chuckling now. "I'll give you a tour—show you how to pull up the door, how to drive in, how to saunter across the street to the station."

Jackson snorted.

The music stopped, then a new record began. "Come on, Clayton," Yvonne said. "This is the only beat slow enough to let me put my hands on those football shoulders." They moved toward the middle of the room. On the sofa behind where they had been standing sat all four young Jacksons, the eight- and ten-year-old poking each other, the eleven-year-old, a pretty girl, smiling as if she were watching a romantic movie, and the oldest boy glaring and stuffing food in his mouth.

"How about you, Jill? You want to dance with the chief? Or are you too tired?" Howard asked.

"No, I'm okay. It's just that I thought I was going to wrap up my case, and instead I hit a dead end."

"Wrap it up? Hey, where are you with this case? I thought you were just getting the feel of it. I didn't realize you were this far."

"You don't want to talk about my case now. I've already made enough use of you with Leon Evans. You don't need me nattering at you during your own party."

"It's okay about Evans," he said, putting a hand on my back and moving out onto the dance floor. My hand barely reached up around his shoulder.

"I didn't want you to think I was just—"

"I said it's okay. Look, I knew Evans was going to hold me up for your talk with him. He wasn't going to get a lot out of me, but he was sure going to get whatever he could. So I set him up." Howard was grinning again. Howard loved any kind of minor sting. He was a terror on April Fool's Day.

"How?"

"I went down to his place right after Morning Meeting, in the squad car. I banged on the door. His goon said he was asleep."

"You knew he'd still be in bed, didn't you?"

"Of course. I've yanked him out of bed more mornings than his mother ever did. But this morning, I told the goon to give him the message that I was there, but to let him sleep."

"So you're even?"

"He may not think so, but I do. And that's what counts. So all that's left of your visit to him last night is your fond thoughts of him when he turns up in a homicide."

The record, "Scotch and Soda," brought back memories of college and high school. I realized that this was the first time I'd danced with Howard. It was such a comfortable feeling that it hadn't seemed novel. It felt normal, like things had always been with Howard and me —like it was before our promotions.

Maybe it was my lack of sleep—I *had* been up all night

—but suddenly I realized how much I had missed Howard—Howard laughing, Howard throwing himself into our bets, our schemes, Howard reveling in winning. I realized a tear was rolling down my cheek.

"Hey, Jill," he said, looking down at me. "What's the matter?"

I swallowed.

He kept his hand on my back and steered me past the food table into the kitchen and out the back door. The air was cold and damp.

"Come on, what is it?" he said, leaning against the wooden railing of the small landing. From it two steps led down to the walkway.

The temptation to explain was fleeting. But I didn't want to chance unsettling things now. This was one of those feelings that was best left unspoken.

"It's not the parking spot, is it?"

"No, Howard. I'm kind of wired from lack of sleep. And—this is going to sound ridiculous—"

"Ridiculous is okay."

"Well, there were all those fake Howards inside. I felt bad that I hadn't been let in on that. I mean, how come I'm not a Howard look-alike?"

Howard laughed. His head rolled back; his red curls shook. "Jill," he said between laughs, "you may think you've grown in importance now that you're a big Homicide detective, but you are still five foot six."

"Five foot seven!"

"A shrimp by any other name . . ."

"Okay, okay. This just isn't my day," I said, grinning in response to his laughter. Howard knew how it irritated me to always be shorter than my friends at work. It made him laugh harder.

When he stopped, he put a hand on my arm. "Okay, Jill, now tell me about your case." That was what the old Howard—this Howard—would have said.

I didn't protest. I told him about my dash into Oak-

land to the Bien Hoa restaurant to find Sam Nguyen.
"With the woman at the cash register, I'm batting one for
three."

Howard waited.

"She told me she doesn't know where Sam Nguyen
lives. I'm sure she's lying about that. She said Sam had
been there at twenty after one every workday this week.
Three witnesses—Palmerston, Cap Danziger, and Jake
Trent—saw him leaving the repair shop at one-thirty the
day Palmerston was killed. So I know she's lying on that
one."

"What's the third?"

"She told me Cap Danziger and Lois Palmerston had
lunch with Sam Nguyen there twice."

"Cap Danziger and Lois Palmerston," he said appraisingly.

"Exactly. I'm sure that was Sam Nguyen's reaction.
I'm willing to bet that was what he told Ralph Palmerston, and what made Palmerston hire Herman Ott. The
only question is why he would have done that. The whole
thing's a riddle, Howard. The guy with the opportunity
has no motive. Five people have Class A motives, but no
chance to cut the brake lines."

"So what are you doing?"

"I don't know. I'm just here at your party."

But Howard was not to be so easily put off. "Maybe
Cap Danziger cut the brake lines and hoped suspicion
would fall on Nguyen. One stone, two birds."

"I accused him—not in those words—and he pointed
out that he would have been rather obvious sidling into
the repair shop and under the car. And, of course, he was
with Palmerston when Nguyen was leaving."

"Hmm."

"I hate to discount Cap Danziger," I said. "He was the
only one of the group that your friend Leon Evans recognized . . . or admitted recognizing," I said slowly.
"Howard, Leon Evans bought two Cadillacs from Cap

Danziger. Danziger himself told me that the reason drug dealers trade with Trent is because of Sam Nguyen."

"And Sam Nguyen," he said, picking up on my thought, "makes over cars."

"I quote, 'secret cargo space—no problem.' "

"So," Howard said, "Sam Nguyen was engineering secret compartments for the Leon Evanses of the world."

"And Cap Danziger knew about it," I said, excited. "He would know, of course."

"And he was blackmailing Sam Nguyen."

"Maybe not for cash. Maybe just for influence. Nguyen forced Trent to rehire Danziger a couple of times when he fired him."

"Whatever. Danziger had a hold on Nguyen."

"Right. And Nguyen could equalize things by doing Cap the favor of cutting Ralph Palmerston's brake lines," I said, almost breathless. "By that, Nguyen disposes of Palmerston at a time when Cap has an unbreakable alibi. And he leaves Lois a wealthy widow free for the taking."

"Now, if you just knew where Sam Nguyen was, huh?"

"But I do, Howard, or at least I can make a good guess. You're not the only one giving a Halloween party."

25

I raced inside, grabbed my purse, and headed out the front door. Howard was right behind me.

"You can't come," I called as I ran. "You're hosting a party. What about your guests?"

"No one will even know I'm gone. They've still got six Howards. I can have a black and white signed out while you're still looking for a parking place by the station."

"You could let me use your garage."

"Can't. I've only got a weekday lease. Mrs. Layton rents it to someone else on the weekends."

A female Mr. Kepple.

We climbed into my car, and I started the engine and pulled out.

"Jill, how do you know there's going to be a party?"

"Adam Thede told me. He's the party giver of the group. It was at his stragglers' breakfast that the scheme was hatched."

"It seems pretty frivolous, your failed schemers going to a party when they should be home worrying."

"Not really, Howard. They're scared, all of them. Their lives had been turned upside down before the murder. The only people they can talk to are each other. Even if this weren't Halloween, they'd want to be together. For them it's just lucky there's an excuse."

"But Sam Nguyen, are you sure he'd want to party with the five of them?"

"Not party so much as keep an eye on them and remind them that they are in this up to their necks and they'd better not turn him in."

I pulled up in front of the station and let Howard out.

He was barely inside the building when a van across the street pulled out. I hung a U and took the spot. A good omen.

Still in my Fairy Godmother's costume, I headed for the parking lot exit, and there I waited. Halloween was not a good time to get a patrol car. I knew it would take Howard longer than usual. I just hoped—recalling Nina and Jeffrey Munson's radical underground connections— that they didn't decide I was getting too close and take Sam Nguyen to a "safe house." If they did, he could disappear for years, maybe forever. I hoped it wasn't too late.

I also hoped it didn't take Howard much longer to sign out the black and white. The night had turned foggy. And the heavy air was cold. It began to cloud my good omen. When Howard pulled up in the car, I gave him Adam Thede's address and said, "I'm beginning to have second thoughts."

"You want me to turn around?"

"No. Keep going. It's just Nguyen's motivation. I mean, it's bad enough that Cap Danziger knows he is creating secret compartments for drug dealers. But if he kills Palmerston, Danziger will know that too. He'll have a lot more to hold over him. Killing Palmerston doesn't get him off the hook at all. It just gets him in deeper."

Howard nodded. "You'd think with friends like Leon Evans, that Nguyen would take the easy and permanent way of disposing of Danziger."

"Damn it. It doesn't make sense. But Nguyen was there."

"Unless the three witnesses were lying and the woman at the restaurant wasn't."

I leaned back against the seat. There was nothing more to say. I ran over the facts of the case again, but they turned up nothing new. I was tempted to sift through them, but being awake all night was catching up with me and my mind was too hazy for details. Instead I let myself think about Howard's party and the gaggle of fake Howards that I had been too short to be a part of.

And when Howard pulled up two houses from Adam Thede's, he said, "So, what now?"

"I'm going in for the killer."

"Wait a minute."

"No. You can't come. Look at you. No one but me would know that you're supposed to be in costume." I pulled up the hood of my Fairy Godmother robe and headed for Thede's house.

Adam Thede's house was a chalet on the downslope of a hill. A brace of tall red devils was leaving. I walked in through the open door. The living room was large, bare of furniture, and dark. In the dim light from the fireplace reptilian-faced monsters gyrated to the dance music. It looked like a scene from hell. I pulled the Fairy Godmother hood closer around my head. Picking up a half-full beer bottle, I made my way through the dancers, eyeing each one, trying to find Sam Nguyen and the Shareholders. But none of the dancers was familiar. A ghoul and a princess sat, arms entwined, on a pillow against the wall, but neither resembled Sam Nguyen.

The dining room was lighter. A bum, a witch, and a packing crate with arms were looking over the buffet. None of the Shareholders here.

Could I have been wrong about this party? I was so sure. Could all of them be lying low elsewhere?

I hesitated. I hadn't seen Adam Thede. Regardless of the validity of my assumptions, he should be here. It was his house. Where was he?

I headed to the kitchen. When I opened the door, I spotted Thede in white chef's garb at the counter, stirring a large bowl of something tan. Next to him was Cap Danziger in a cavalier's costume looking down at a small, dark-haired figure in an Oriental jacket.

None of them moved. Bracing myself in front of the door to the dining room, I glanced quickly around the kitchen. The only other door led onto the deck. From there it had to be a thirty-foot drop.

I looked at the back of the Oriental jacket, at the blunt-cut dark hair. I thought of the fake Howards. Pushing my hood back, I said, "Nina Munson, I arrest you for the murder of Ralph Palmerston."

She whirled toward me and stared. No one moved. Then she grabbed the bowl out of Thede's hands and flung the gook in my face.

Frantically I scooped the thick sauce out of my eyes. When I could see, Nina was already on the deck railing.

"Don't!" I yelled.

She looked at me a moment, and jumped.

I didn't need to hear more than her scream to know that this time she had miscalculated.

26

Nina Munson wasn't dead, but she wouldn't walk for a while either.

The wait for the ambulance, taking the statements, and all the paperwork took hours. I had promised Howard I would answer every one of his questions when I finished, and he, according to our custom, would take me out for dinner at Priester's Restaurant to celebrate my collar. But that would have to wait.

As I drove home, the darkness was lifting. Soon it would be dawn. I pulled up in front of the Kepple house, walked around back, and as I had last night, took off only my jacket and slacks before crawling into my sleeping bag.

In the few seconds before I fell asleep, I thought about setting the alarm. I'd promised Howard I'd see him later. I didn't want to sleep through till morning.

But I needn't have worried. The whirring of Mr. Kepple's electric edger jolted me out of the bag. Why did this man have to do his raucous gardening at the crack of dawn? This time I *would* complain. I was completely out of the bag before I realized it was four in the afternoon.

Muttering a silent apology to Mr. Kepple, I headed for the shower. And at quarter to five I was pulling up in front of Howard's house. At least, I thought, by now the place will be cleaned and back to normal.

But as Howard opened the door, I saw that I was wrong. The living room resembled nothing so much as the returned garment room at California Costumery. The empty back end of the horse leaned against a sofa, a plumed helmet propped on its tail. Ellis's compost heap covered the rest of the sofa and littered the floor. A Marie Antoinette wig lay next to a bald pate, next to a cotton tail, next to a bear's head wearing glasses with the eyes popping out. My pumpkin was sporting a Howard wig and a patrol officer's cap. And beneath, between, and on top of the costumes were wadded napkins, paper plates with dried clumps of food, and beer cans—cans that held enough beer to satisfy an average American town till the turn of the century.

"I started with the kitchen," Howard said in way of explanation.

"I hate to think what shape that must be in then."

He just shook his head and made his way through the litter to the sofa and pushed the accumulated debris to the floor. "Ellis was supposed to help clean up. He's too wasted to move. The rest of the guys . . . well, I guess I don't need to go into that." Howard's complaints about his ever-changing cadre of roommates had paralleled mine about my ex-husband. We had, at times, had yearning discussions about caves in the Himalayas.

"About my case," I said to distract him, "what do you want to know?"

He perked up. "The footprints under Lois Palmerston's window. Who made them? I've been trying to figure that out all day."

"Want to guess?"

"Jeffrey Munson? You said he wore running shoes. He seemed like a skulker."

I laughed. "No. Actually, there was no need for any of the five suspects to peek in Lois's window. It would have been dangerous for them to park in front of the house and creep around in the bushes. If they'd wanted to find out about Lois, they would have called, or rung the bell. They hadn't been watching her house all night. They didn't know there had been no lights on. If any of them had come by, they would have assumed she'd gone to bed early. The only person who was watching the house, and who was being driven crazy by the lights being off, was my friend Billy Kershon."

"The kid across the street?"

"Right. I saw him that day in his shorts and running shoes. Even then he was keeping an eye on the house. He spotted me right away. He charged over and asked me about the case. And I"—I sighed—"told him that I could use all the help I could get."

Howard laughed. "Your own personal deputy, huh?"

"When I take him on his tour of the station, I'll have to remind him that private investigators shouldn't go around breaking the law, even to help the police."

Howard shifted the half-horse's tail and stretched his long legs, resting his feet on a white styrofoam orb the size of a medicine ball. (I remembered a woman had come to the party as a snowman. Apparently, she had left without her middle snowball.) "But, Jill, how did you know the killer was Nina Munson? When you got out of the car, I was still figuring it to be Sam Nguyen."

"Well, the killer had to be Sam Nguyen, but it couldn't have been Sam Nguyen. So the only possibility was someone who looked like Sam. It was your fake Howards that gave me the idea. Even knowing that I was at a costume party, when I saw the first one I thought it was you."

"You did?" Howard looked insulted.

"Well, it was your house; I expected to see you here. I was talking to Pereira, not thinking about you. And the fake Howard looked enough like you from the back to pass. There was no reason to assume it wasn't you."

"Nina Munson and Sam Nguyen, do they look that much alike?"

"From the back. They're both short. They have very

dark, blunt-cut hair. At Trent Cadillac, Nina wore white overalls and a white jacket. And when Ralph Palmerston, Cap Danziger, and Jake Trent saw her back as she was leaving the shop, there was no reason for them to assume they'd seen anyone but Sam Nguyen. They saw someone who looked like Sam, in a place where Sam should be. Without giving it a thought, they assumed it was Sam."

"But what about the time. You said by that time of day Sam was always at lunch."

"True. Sam knew that and the Vietnamese restaurant knew it. But no one at Trent Cadillac held Sam accountable for his time. He came and went as he pleased. If he chose to have lunch late one day no one thought anything of it. And besides, with Ralph Palmerston throwing a tantrum, Jake Trent and Cap Danziger were so busy trying to placate him, they weren't worrying about the time."

"So Nina planned it all alone?"

"So she says. And I believe her. She said she'd had enough of hassling with collaborators. She was used to making her own decisions and facing the consequences. She'd taken chances before. She was the one who was expelled from college for taking on the dean. When the five Shareholders concocted the scheme, it was just party talk. Nina was the one who decided to make it reality. She called Lois: she got her out here. And the others were swept along into the operation."

Howard nodded. "But cutting the brake lines: it's such a masculine kind of crime."

"That's what appealed to Nina. She had helped Jeffrey enough with cars to know where the brake lines were, and she had a firm hand from sewing to make the punctures with."

"But Jill, she still had to get to the car."

I brushed the potato chip rubble from the arm of the couch. "That was the hard part. Fortunately for her, Palmerston's car was parked near the back door of the shop. Getting to the car wasn't really dangerous. She hadn't committed any crime yet. She was just a person dressed in white overalls. If someone had spotted her then, she could have turned around and walked out.

"The chanciest moment was at the car itself, getting in position to make the perforations. But once she was doing the work, she was just another pair of white-overalled legs sticking out. No one would look twice at that. That's what you see in the repair shop. And when she finished, all she had to do was keep her back to the area where the customers wait. That's when Danziger spotted her and he, Trent, and Palmerston assumed she was Sam Nguyen."

"But what about Cap Danziger? Didn't he recognize Nina?"

"He denies it. At the time he assumed she was Sam Nguyen. If he did see through the disguise—which he also denies—it wasn't till much later."

"But he knew that Sam Nguyen would be at lunch when he saw Nina in the repair shop. When he heard that the brake lines had been cut, didn't that make him suspicious?"

"You'd think it might. But, as he told me, he didn't want to ponder unpleasant topics like murder. He isn't a man who likes to get his hands dirty." I leaned forward. "Cap is the one who told me Sam always went to lunch at one o'clock. If he'd been involved with Nina, or even realized how she'd killed Ralph Palmerston, he never would have given me such an incriminating piece of information. He didn't want me to solve this murder any more than any of the other Shareholders did. To them the murder itself was peripheral. What they feared was that if I kept digging I'd discover the Shareholders scheme and find out what Ralph Palmerston knew about each of them and it would all become public knowledge. That's why Cap kept tabs on me. That's why he filed the complaint."

Howard pulled a curly red wig from the space between the sofa cushions. Eyeing it with disgust, he tossed it onto the pile of beer cans. "Still, Nina Munson was one cool cookie. I can see why the 'Sam Nguyen' Palmerston called to didn't stop to talk."

I laughed. "That must have been one truly awful moment for Nina."

"It all sounds pretty cold-blooded. Did she kill Palmerston just for revenge?"

"It was a combination of things. Revenge—after all, she'd taken care of Lois for years, and like Jeffrey said, all that time Nina never admitted that Lois could do wrong. So when Lois dropped her and Nina finally realized how she'd been used all those years, it was a very big shock. But she also killed Palmerston to save Jeffrey from being exposed; and to save Jeffrey's business. She got twenty-five percent of the profits. She couldn't live without that money. So it was a mixture of revenge, protection, and self-preservation."

"Very practical lady," Howard said. Then he grinned in anticipation. "What about Sam Nguyen?"

"Can't wait to get your hands on him, huh?"

"I don't want to appear greedy—"

I laughed. That was exactly how he appeared.

"I don't want to appear greedy," Howard insisted, "but Cap Danziger had something on him, and when you find that out, I'm planning to squeeze Nguyen till he spits out every drop of information on every drug dealer in the city."

"An unappetizing picture."

Dusk was beginning to fall. In it, the room looked even more depressing. "Despite that picture, I'm ready for dinner. Giving you an excuse to get out of here is the least I can do."

"The least?" Howard was sitting up straight. I knew that look of his. I'd seen it when he told me about his scheme to even things out with Leon Evans. I waited.

"Jill," he said, slowly, "I know you really wanted my parking spot. A garage space would have been very useful to you."

"Mmm."

"Particularly on Monday mornings. You're never on time Mondays."

"Mmm?"

"I realize that figuring out my costume was a little too hard for you."

"Howard!"

"Okay. But I could still let you have that garage on Monday mornings."

"For what in return?"

He glanced around the room. "The kitchen's already half done. Only the counters and the floor and the stuff caked on the icebox door are left. Oh, and the walls—you know what that aerosol hors d'oeuvre stuff can do."

When I didn't respond, he said, "I'm just asking for help, not for you to take on the whole job. I know this isn't exactly your field of expertise."

He looked truly desperate. I laughed. "Make it Mondays and Fridays and you're on. But we don't start till after dinner."